AN AMERICAN MEMORY

AN AMERICAN MEMORY

A Novel by Eric Larsen

ANCHOR BOOKS

DOUBLEDAY

NEW YORK   LONDON   TORONTO   SYDNEY   AUCKLAND

AN ANCHOR BOOK

PUBLISHED BY DOUBLEDAY

a division of Bantam Doubleday Dell Publishing Group, Inc.
666 Fifth Avenue, New York, New York 10103

ANCHOR BOOKS, DOUBLEDAY, and the portrayal of an anchor
are trademarks of Doubleday, a division of Bantam Doubleday
Dell Publishing Group, Inc.

Grateful acknowledgment is made to the following publications, in which a
number of sections of this book first appeared: *The South Dakota Review*
(section Eight under the title "Malcolm's Dream: My Father Goes to War");
New England Review and Bread Loaf Quarterly (section Eleven under the
title "Visitor"); *The North American Review* (section Five under the title
"Babies"); *The Ohio Review* (section Seven under the title "Hannah"); *Prairie
Schooner* (sections Four and Nine under the titles "The Photographs" and
"The Lake"; copyright © 1980 by the University of Nebraska Press; reprinted
by permission of the University of Nebraska Press). Epigraph excerpted
from "Grandparents" from *Life Studies* by Robert Lowell. Copyright© 1956 by
Robert Lowell. Reprinted by permission of Farrar, Straus & Giroux Inc.

An American Memory was originally published in hardcover by Algonquin
Books of Chapel Hill in association with Taylor Publishing Company in 1988.
The Anchor Books edition is published by arrangement with Algonquin Books.

Library of Congress Cataloging-in-Publication Data
Larsen, Eric, 1941–
    An American memory: a novel / by Eric Larsen.
    1st Anchor Books ed.
        p.   cm.
    Originally published: Chapel Hill, N.C.:
    Algonquin Books of Chapel Hill, 1988.
    ISBN 0-385-26255-8
    I. Title.
[PS3562.A732A8   1989]   89-33124
813'.54—dc20   CIP

For my daughters,
FLYNN AND GAVIN

the nineteenth century, tired of children, is gone.
They're all gone into a world of light; the farm's my own.

—Robert Lowell, *Life Studies*

AN AMERICAN MEMORY

MALCOLM REINER'S NOTEBOOK

*History has no voice. When time stops,
there is only quietness; the figures of
history speak in silence.*

ONE

(1881–1923)

I

In my early thirties, at a time when I am especially frightened of death, I will have a dream of my maternal grandfather; he will appear before me one night as a skeleton draped in a theatrically flowing grave shroud. When he sees me staring at him, he will greet me by bowing elegantly from the waist, one arm sweeping slowly before him. Nothing further will happen except that, after taking his bow, he will stand once again and gaze directly at me. The dream will take only a moment; it will be little more than an image seen through a briefly opened shutter.

In this glimpse of my grandfather from beyond the grave, I will be aware of a quality of foolish and macabre merriment unlike anything that accompanied his long and more dour life. In my brief dream-encounter I will see that colorful gems are set in glittering rows on the fleshless bones of my grandfather's fingers. I will watch his wide mouth leer at me with its skeleton's idiotic, inflexible grin. And I will see, nestled snugly inside his empty skull, twin rolls of theater tickets which can be unwound, as in a ticket dispenser, by pulling the strings of tickets out through the shadowy sockets of my grandfather's eyes.

.

The vision in itself does not frighten me, but when I awaken I become aware that it has stirred memories that have settled deeply within me. Half unwillingly, I am pulled backward toward them.

.

My grandfather, dressed in a dark suit, with gleaming black shoes, takes a green ticket that I hold up to him in my hand. His voice is humorless but grudgingly approving, and he calls me "little man." There is the smell of fresh popcorn, and the muffled sound of its popping. The woman behind the high glass counter says something to my grandfather, smiles at me and bends down, her face looming toward me and bringing with it the scent of perfume. She gives me something wrapped in waxy paper, pushing it into my hand. This is during wartime, and my father is away. Inside the auditorium I sit alone, surrounded by rows of plush, empty seats, waiting for other people to come in at last by ones and twos and find their places. The ornate auditorium, dark and prolix with the garnish and trim of another century, is muffled and silent. People begin to enter at the rear. I listen to the newcomers speaking in low uncertain voices.

.

On Saturday afternoons, before the box office opens for the matinee, I go with my grandfather backstage, where it is necessary for him to adjust electrical switches and on occasion to bring out new rolls of green tickets. The theater backstage is constructed of bare wood, with exposed beams high under the wooden roof. On some of the walls hang tattered playbills and colored posters from years like 1894 and 1908. Against other walls lean stacks of stiff showboards for movies, having at one time stood as sandwich boards on the sidewalk in front of the theater. Sandbags rest near the edge of the dusty floor, and tied to their cinched necks are ropes that curve upward to pulleys in the darkness near the rafters. Stairs lead to three small rooms on a balcony midway up one wall; my grand-father explains that these were dressing rooms for actors. As usual, he expresses no joy in the things he tells me.

The opening of the stage is plugged up now by the square movie screen, held upright, like a billboard, with wooden braces and struts. I walk toward it until I stand directly behind it; I imagine that through its taut skin I can see the rows of empty seats in the auditorium facing me and, in turn, that I can be seen on the stage. I am dwarfed by the vast white screen, which stands there like an enormous eye. When my grandfather, preoccupied for a moment with some-thing else, sees where I am standing, he calls out angrily at once, in a sharp voice, forbidding me to touch it.

·

My grandfather lived for eighty-four years; the significance is how little in that time he changed. There was in him from the beginning a sullenness that prevented him from responding to the evocativeness and excitement of the radi-cally changing world around him. He was looked upon by most as practical and assertive, but in truth he was subtly resentful toward all things in a peculiarly joyless way that kept him passive and narrow. My grandfather was insuscep-tible to the abstract sense of wonder without which joy is not possible. His body was small and sturdy; in middle age it became heavy with a stout Edwardian portliness. His face possessed a handsome severity of expression that gave to his portraits throughout his life a look of assurance and stern power. But in his spirit, underneath this solid cover of flesh, was hidden the thin and unsparing rigidness of the Calvinist zealot or country puritan, in his case without even the root of a vital faith to nourish or give it the luxury of meaning. My grandfather was a man who went through his life without grace of imagination. Stolid, purposeful, sternly comforting as he may have seemed on the outside, the wind blew through my grandfather's bones.

·

He kept an office on the mezzanine level of the theater, a small room with a single high window like a turret window in a castle. The room was large enough to hold a desk and chair, a filing cabinet, a small old-fashioned sofa. Two shelves over the desk held bound ledgers; below them, on a smaller shelf, stood six glasses, a quart of whiskey, and a pitcher for water. Tucked in one corner was a low iron safe squatting on four feathered talons, each clutching beneath it a dull iron ball. In this small room, in the middle of the mornings, my grandfather wrote checks, balanced his ledgers, wrote out booking orders for films: cartoons, romances, musical comedies, always accompanied by newsreels that showed the progress of battles on the far sides of the earth.

When he was inside his office, the door would stand open; a shaft of light from his desk lamp would fall across the red carpeting of the mezzanine where the staircase turned up toward the darkness of the balcony seats. In the auditorium, two cleaning ladies would vacuum between the rows of seats, their machines attached to long black cords plugged in under the skirt of the stage. They would sweep up spilled popcorn, pieces of candy, crumpled wrappers of various kinds. Under the seats they would find lost coins, dropped scarves, gloves, handkerchiefs, sometimes wallets or valued personal objects, necklaces, trinkets, jeweled rings, sometimes dollar bills.

•

There is a memory that stays with me in which it seems always to be February or March, the months of chill gray light, and in which the time seems always to be the same vacant, slow hour of midmorning. Outdoors, the snow is turning to slush; it falls in wet clumps from the black branches of trees, and, in the streets, the tires of cars leave deep ruts in the slush, which then fill with icy water. In this memory there is a cold buffeting wind, heavy and strong with a cutting dampness, under a sky that is low and gray.

Inside the theater, I feel aimless and confined, burdened with empty time. I embark upon a circular pattern, which compulsively I trace over and over. I climb up the stairway past my grandfather's open door, then continue along the muffled carpeting up into the chill emptiness of the balcony. I cross through the darkness of the balcony; descend the opposite staircase; move through the wan gray daylight of the main lobby; then re-ascend silently past my grandfather's open door. I make this identical journey six, eight, perhaps ten or a dozen times, running as quickly as I am able without breaking my silence or alerting my grandfather, traveling in circles through the darkness of the hollow old theater.

When I am exhausted, I climb to the top row of the balcony and find my way into a center seat, beneath the square holes cut into the wall of the projectionist's booth. The auditorium is dark, illuminated only by the dim glow of the exit signs over the doors. Waiting for my breath to calm, I gaze down through this great volume of historical emptiness, able to see only vaguely the pale image of the screen standing behind its thin translucent curtain. As my wild heartbeat slowly quiets, silence closes in around me. I am enclosed inside a vast dark space free of sound, of motion, perhaps even of time. I wait. I seem to sense only a great silence. Then at last I begin to hear the sounds of the wind from outdoors. There is a dull buffet against the wooden roof. From somewhere backstage comes a subdued, hesitant moan. Then the wind gets caught under a roofboard, or tries to come in at a barred doorway, and I hear a high rising whistle, a small voice thin with unspeakable weariness, a sound that comes from the far distance of the dead past, palely wavering, tenuous, as frail as a thread.

II

I am not a part of the history that follows. When these events occurred, I did not exist, I had not been imagined, I was not dreamed of. I am excluded entirely from them.

What strikes me most vividly about these recorded memories is that they have been stopped by time, that they are entirely static, that they can never change, not in the slightest way whatsoever.

No one populates these events. The characters in them are dead.

1

My grandfather is born in a white clapboard farmhouse five miles outside the town of West Tree, Minnesota, sixteen years after the close of the Civil War.

·

A quarter of a mile from the farmhouse a railroad passes by, named for the famous race horse Dan Patch. At the place where the dirt road crosses the railway, near the small station house, there stands a country tavern. It is shaded by a wide cottonwood, a tree as dense and luxuriant as those seen in photographs made by Matthew Brady during the period of the Civil War.

.

Along the railroad is a farm with a large stock of horses. The barn in which the animals are kept is painted in broad red and white stripes, and one night this barn burns to the ground, consumed by flames that stretch and leap high against the black sky. It is believed that vagrants walking along the railroad took shelter there for the night and dropped an ash into the hay.

The fire occurred in late March. My grandfather, awakened from his sleep, ran to help move the terrified horses from their stalls. At this time my grandfather was ten years old. His bare feet, as he ran, broke through the skins of ice that covered the water in the ruts of the dirt road.

.

When he is seventeen, my grandfather leaves the farm. In the deep silence past midnight one week in June, he jumps from his second floor window onto dew-laden grass and steals away quietly under the shadows of elms. He goes to West Tree, Minnesota. There he finds work as an apprentice to a house painter. The year is 1898. A man named Ephraim LeRoy, in the shed next to his house in West Tree, is attempting to construct an automobile.

2

When my grandfather is nineteen years old, he joins a group of amateur thespians. One evening each week its members meet in the front parlor of a rooming house to read aloud from the works of Shakespeare. Normally this meeting occurs on Sunday evenings. The rooming house, on the north edge of town, stands across from the red brick college buildings, two in number, that rise alone and stark on a bare, unprotected hill.

·

The leader of the thespians is a high school teacher named Rebecca Kerndon, who lives in the second floor of the house. One of her students lives there also, a girl in her first year of high school named Charlotte Sitney. During vacations and at the end of each school year, Charlotte Sitney returns to her parents' farmhouse twelve miles outside of West Tree. On more than one occasion, my grandfather rents a trap and conveys her that distance.

In time, Charlotte Sitney will become my grandmother.

·

After the readings on Sunday nights, Rebecca Kerndon serves apple cider and pastries to the members of her group. A fire burns on the grate. A hooked rug lies on the wooden floor. On the coldest nights of the winter, frost forms in fernlike patterns on the front windowpanes of the parlor.

·

One afternoon in May of the year 1900 my grandfather calls on Charlotte Sitney at the rooming house. The two of them stroll together through the town toward the trees that line the low banks of the river. The day is fine, with a blue sky, a light warm breeze. It is one of the occasions on which Ephraim LeRoy takes out his homemade automobile. On the town's main street he passes by my grandfather and Charlotte Sitney. The small machine with its large wheels and high seat is spidery and frail, with a tiller to steer it. It frightens a passing horse. The horse rears, tosses its head, and shows the whites of its eyes.

3

My grandfather associates himself with a theatrical group that travels from one small town to another during the winter season, offering performances of the plays of Shakespeare. My grandfather plays roles in *The Two Gentlemen of Verona* and *Julius Caesar*. He appears in *Much Ado About Nothing*. Later he is given the role of Mercutio in *Romeo and Juliet*. Before he gives up acting, he will have played Shylock, Hamlet, and Romeo.

·

In the mornings when the troupe is on the road, there is thin ice in the pitchers of cold water on the hotel dressers. Outdoors, the streets are unpaved, rutted with hard-frozen mud. Fine snow sometimes drifts over them. In the evenings my grandfather's eyes are severely darkened, his cheekbones rouged, his lips painted red. Onstage, he delivers his lines with dramatic rises and falls of his voice. He clenches his fists. He extends his arms in front of his body to indicate passion, and he turns his face upward toward the top of the gallery and holds his gaze fixed there for considerable periods of time. When he is not acclaimed as he would wish, he learns slowly to despise his audiences.

During the time that he is an actor, my grandfather does not give up housepainting.

4

He appears onstage for the last time when he is twenty-eight years old. Much earlier than that, he sees Charlotte Sitney appear as the female lead in a high school class play.

The audiences are warmly taken by her physical beauty, her confidence and her charm, and they applaud her with enthusiasm. My grandfather is pierced by jealousy and anger. A possessive youth, he is tormented by seeing my grandmother expose herself willingly onstage to the responsive gaze of so many eager eyes. In subsequent private conversations with her, he forbids her to act. She complies with his wish, believing that she will lose his love if she does not, but for forty years she continues to believe that she possesses an unjustly thwarted calling for the stage.

·

My grandfather, becoming now a young man of some reputation, begins to acquire the outward appearance of sullenness and dour gravity that he will possess, to greater or lesser extents, for the rest of his life.

He is said by some to be excessively severe of expression and manner, at times even surly, although customarily these faults are forgiven him, especially by romantic admirers, as being deemed appropriate to the earnestness of his talent and youth.

5

My grandfather offers marriage to Charlotte Sitney, but her father finds strenuous objection. In this objection he is firm. My grandfather is insufficiently stable. He possesses no savings. He holds inadequate assets. He owns no house, farm, or business. He shows little inclination toward making himself more reliable and solid than he appears to be already at this point in his life.

·

In the hushed time past midnight in March of 1907, my grandfather places a ladder under a second floor window of a clapboard farmhouse. Charlotte Sitney descends it. The two of them hurry a quarter of a mile under the branches of bare trees to the place where my grandfather has tethered a horse with a buggy. There is mud on the roads from the early spring thawing. Although gouts of it cling to the slowly turning rims of the wheels and to the horse's hooves, the mud is not deep enough to impede their drive to West Tree. A thin crescent moon descends in the west, obscured at times by clouds.

III

The sexual life between the young couple did not become what might have been expected or wished. As if to confirm the extent of this failure, the birth of their daughter a year after the marriage was accompanied by prolonged and unexpected pain, considerable physical danger to mother and child, and intense terror. Afterwards the young mother, in spite of her outward appearance of a strong constitution, suffered from a case of extended anemia. In the year following the birth, she developed as well palpitations of the heart, bronchial asthma, and fluctuating symptoms of neurasthenia. She was cautioned for her own safety not to become pregnant again, and this first daughter, who in the course of time would become my mother, was to remain her only child.

Although slow to recover from her illness, my grandmother retained her physical beauty. She was thought to appear especially charming when with her child, and she took great pleasure at being seen with her in public.

·

After his marriage, my grandfather set out independently in business. He began to do work in the interiors of houses as well as on the exteriors. New houses were being built in the growing town, and in them he did painting, woodworking, and paperhanging. He was said to be especially skilled with varnish and the staining of fine wood. He hired three work-men under him and took on a partner, forming a small com-pany. He performed a role in a traveling production of *Love's Labours Lost*, another in *Macbeth*. A small number of addi-tional roles followed after these, and then his acting career came to an end. For a short time there was a question about his relationship with a young actress from St. Paul. This was the first of several occasions when one of my grandparents was to accuse the other of infidelity, usually without explicit foundation, but with intense jealousy and bitter resentment.

.

In 1910 my grandfather bought his first automobile. One day in late April the small family drove five miles to the farm where my grandfather was born. My mother was two years old. Wearing a ruffled spring bonnet and bundled in warm clothing, she was placed on the grass at the farm and pho-tographs were taken while two white rabbits and a fat red hen came to take pieces of corn from her hand. On the way home, the family crossed the railroad track and stopped for lunch at the country tavern under the budding cottonwood tree. To those in the tavern—including the two or three pas-sengers waiting for the train to St. Paul—the young family appeared happy, prosperous, even fashionable and somewhat daring. They were watched from the windows of the tavern as they departed in their automobile, their clothing protected under dusters, caps on their heads, the child held firmly on her mother's lap. A year later the tavern was to burn. In 1933 the railroad was to fall into disuse, weeds and grass growing in the roadbed, and the small crossroads station was to be abandoned. In 1957 the foundation stones of the tavern could still be found under the tall grass of an untilled portion of land. I know this because in that year, when I was sixteen years old, I stopped there with my grandfather one day in the summer and felt for the stones with my hands. The spreading cottonwood tree was to be gone without any trace.

·

In 1913 my grandfather traveled to St. Paul by that same train to meet with a theatrical producer named Sam Cornish and a small group of men interested in becoming backers or partners. The property in West Tree that they proposed to buy was known as Castle Auditorium; after its purchase the name was changed to Riverside Theater. The corporate ownership was known initially as Cornish Theatricals, but as the years went by, my grandfather was to buy out the other partners one by one until in 1928 he possessed title to the property independently. In 1933 the name Cornish disappeared from the legal papers.

·

At first the theater continued to book road shows and repertory groups; it showed moving pictures one night a week. By 1915, moving pictures occupied it eight or ten nights a month. In 1922 a screen was permanently installed and the auditorium was converted into a moving picture theater. By this time, my grandfather no longer wore workman's clothing and was no longer associated with his business in housepainting and interior finishing. He could be seen on the main street of the town during daytime hours wearing brown suits with buttoned vests, a gold watch chain visible across the front. He smoked cigars. On warm evenings he would often emerge from the theater and stand at the curb outside its

doors, while, inside, the paying audience would sit in their
rows of seats amid ornate surroundings and watch the movies
play themselves out. Mygrandfather at such times would cut
a fresh cigar with a small silver clipper, light it with a wooden
match, then stand gazing across the street or down toward
the slowly flowing river as he smoked. After a time, he would
turn and go back in through the lobby doors of the theater.
He had grown a carefully trimmed mustache, which heightened the handsome severity of his appearance.

·

Early in the marriage, my grandmother developed a mor-
bid fear that her child would die or be seriously injured. She
feared that the girl might contract a fatal disease, fall and
break her skull, or that she might be trampled under the
hooves of a horse or choke to death on a piece of food. Perhaps these fears and the extreme protectiveness that resulted
from them were caused by her inability to have another child,
or by the depth of her conviction that to give birth again was
impossible without the certain risk of her own life. She clung
protectively to the child and yet at moments seemed also to
resent her deeply, just as at times she expressed resentment
toward her husband, giving as reason most often that it was
he who stood as an obstacle to a career in acting of her own.
She was quick to lash out in anger for no apparent reason or
on the slightest pretext, and for a long period in these years
of her marriage she came to be known for possessing a violent
temper.

She continued, however, to be praised for her beauty,
but it was important to my grandfather that such praise be
given tactfully and with careful measure, so as not to create
offense or seem mere flattery, invoking inadvertently either
my grandmother's spirited pride or her uncontainable rage.

My grandfather himself was not always skilled at keeping his own temper when accused of unfairness of one kind or another by his wife, especially if the accusation had to do with infidelity or happened to be made in the presence of others. It was frequently impossible for him to find justice in the charges she made or to accept without anger what he perceived as her attempt to embarrass him in public. In his need, he talked about her behind her back, as a means of explaining to acquaintances the necessity for caution.

.

As one means of placating his wife—or perhaps also because he shared her fears—my grandfather supported his wife adamantly in a program of protective measures toward their child. By the time my mother was four years old, these rules were well developed and adhered to. Only rarely was she permitted to play with other children, for fear of contagious diseases. She was in no case permitted to go outdoors alone. She was not permitted to have a red wagon or any toy with wheels that was intended to be ridden. She was not allowed to have roller skates or a two-wheeled scooter. In winter she was not permitted to ice skate. She could not ride ponies or horses. When eating, she was required always to swallow a bite of food before she was allowed to take a drink from a glass. She was allowed neither popcorn nor pieces of hard candy, and lollipops were permitted only so long as she remained seated while eating them and resisted the temptation to chew them. Her stools were watched with careful scrutiny, and once a week she was given castor oil.

Through this kind of regimen, she became a quiet and placable child, obedient to her parents, however inwardly recalcitrant she may have been. In her lifetime she was never to leave her birthplace of West Tree, Minnesota, other than for short periods of time, and her parents themselves, in their later years, were to move again into the same household with her and live there until their deaths. This child, their only daughter, was to marry, have three children, and die in the year 1974 at the age of sixty-six, eighteen years after the death of her mother, fourteen after that of her own eldest child, nine after that of her father, and eight after that of her husband, leaving that particular stage considerably emptied.

·

As a young child, with her fair skin, dark eyes, and the black hair that formed short curls around her face, my mother attracted a great deal of attention and drew comments of praise for her appearance. It was remarked frequently how very much she looked like her mother and how much she shared her beauty. Often the two of them could be seen in a back row of the theater, the child sitting on the mother's lap, watching together the films of Mary Pickford or Lillian Gish on the square screen flanked by its ornate black buntings. By this time, my grandfather had converted a suite of rooms above the lobby of the theater into living quarters for the family. After a movie in the evening, my grandmother would escort her small daughter quickly up the carpeted stairway, then through a side door on the mezzanine landing, and tuck her safely into bed. Downstairs, when the last customer had left the theater, my grandfather would lock the doors. He would turn out the lights. He would come upstairs.

·

One warm evening in May of 1923, my grandfather stepped out onto the sidewalk in front of the theater, and, instead of remaining there in his usual proprietary stance, chose to stroll down the hill a block and a half to the river. He went slowly, with the comfortable leisure of a man upon whom time is not pressing.

At the main street, standing on the curb across from the town square, he paused, drew a cigar from an inside pocket of his brown suit, passed its length once under his nose, struck a wooden match, and lit the tobacco. He was alone on the street except for three or four men half a block away sitting on the wooden bench outside the front of the drugstore. Other shops were closed, business hours over. My grandfather did, however, stand and watch a merchant on the other side of the square as he locked the door of a stationer's shop and then set out on his way home, crossing the town square on a diagonal, passing the wooden scaffolding in its center where a stone monument was being raised.

When the merchant was out of sight, my grandfather stepped from the curb, crossed the empty main street with its paving of oiled wooden blocks, and strolled the additional half block to the river. There he leaned with his forearms on the iron railing of the bridge and for a considerable time remained motionless, except for the small movements when he raised his cigar to his lips and, drawing on it, intensified the glow of its red ash in the gathering dusk.

At this time in its history, the river had not grown brown nor had its smell become offensive. A small open boat was tethered at the base of a stone retaining wall not far downstream from the bridge. It could be reached by an iron stairway fixed to the stone wall, descending to the surface of the water, where the boat tugged gently against the pull of the current. My grandfather stood on the bridge gazing down at the river.

How long he remained there, I don't know. He is dead; perhaps he can be imagined to be there still. The evening is calm and hushed. The smoke from his cigar rises over his head, and he listens to the quiet sounds of the town around him—a dog barking somewhere, the voices of children playing in the distance. He hears the evening train coming into the station a block west of the river. The abbreviated squeal of the steel brakes, the rushing release of steam, voices shouting briefly. More hissing of steam, another shout, the deep thrust of the pistons, then the sounds of the train moving through the town and diminishing gradually into the distance, the whistle blowing at the crossings, each time farther away. Then, as if it is late and in a hurry, the motorcar that is used as a taxi crosses the bridge toward the station, turns a corner, continues out of sight.

There is no more movement. The warm spring evening settles again slowly into a hushed calm. After a time, while my grandfather stands at the rail, a lone pedestrian crosses the bridge toward town, carrying a suitcase.

NOTEBOOK

*Some time after his own father's death,
and carrying the guilt of it behind him like
a trailing cloud of dark gauze, my father
came with his family from New York to the
plains of the Middle West.*

*Now, more than half a century later,
the significance of that family migration
must be seen as purely historical, possessing only those limited meanings that can
continue to reside in a single moment long
abandoned in time.*

*Frequently, though, I think of the
journey in terms that are more strictly
personal: I think of it as the occasion of
my father's first coming westward to meet
with me in the unsought and gratuitous
encounter of my own birth.*

TWO

(1882–1925)

Prologue

i

My father's father was born in the year 1882 on the tall-grass prairies of Iowa. From his own distinguished and Norwegian-immigrant father he inherited extremely long bones, a towering brow, deep-set eyes, and an intense, deeply unquestioning faith in Christ that sequestered him effectively from the mainstream of the changing world into which he was born.

From the beginning, this son of the nineteenth century's end was exceptional in the display of his devotion. It became apparent from a time early in his youth that my grandfather would, like his own eminent and reverend father, give over his earthly life to furthering the work of the Lord.

•

In 1905, when he was twenty-three years old, my grandfather entered a course of seminary study in St. Paul, Minnesota. By this time he had finished college and had spent three years, novitiatelike, as a teacher of Latin and of Roman history in remote rural townships in the far reaches of the Dakotas.

On completion of his seminary studies, in the year 1908, he was ordained. Immediately afterward, he became pastor of a congregation in a small town near the northern border of Iowa, and it was here that he took as his wife a local young woman of modest background, upright character, and plain if undeniable beauty. Within the first year of their marriage, she presented him with their firstborn child, a son, baptized Harold after his father's own Christian name.

There is a photograph of the three of them, taken in the front parlor of their house in the small town in Iowa and dated 1909. The father is seated in a high-backed chair. His high oval face is serious, proprietary, and unsmiling. The infant, dressed in a flowing white baptismal gown of handworked lace, sits on his father's lap, gazing with innocent round eyes into the lens of the camera. The mother stands behind the chair, one hand resting lightly and with a respectful modesty on the broad shoulder of her seated husband.

The infant in the white baptismal gown—years later—is to become my father. And therefore I know the strange truth that this small infant with the round eyes, sitting innocently in white on his father's lap in the parlor of a frame house in Iowa in the year 1909, will grow into a man who is to be tormented and paralyzed for almost the whole of his life by emotional contradiction, unexpressed terror, and a fierce, unresolved anger.

It is interesting to wonder how this will come to be. I know that my grandfather, the stern man in the high-backed chair, is to die, quite suddenly, of an illness of the lungs, in January of 1923. What I believe is that something will die also within my own father at that same time: something within my father will seize, become frozen, in the year 1923, when he has reached the age of thirteen, altering and marking him for the remainder of his life.

ii

Few people, I imagine, could succeed in living their lives
with such a degree of emotional rigidness as my father suc-
ceeded in living his; it seems to me now, looking back from
the vantage point of my own adulthood, that my father was
a nearly perfected master of guardedness and repression.
Throughout his life, he kept major parts of his emotional
life securely buried and deeply in hiding—from his children,
from others outside the family, perhaps from himself as well.

The years of his childhood, for example: My father made
a largely successful effort to live as though no childhood had
preceded his adult life. For as long as I knew him, he discour-
aged or denied questions about his early years; with scorn,
aloofness, and impatience, he stifled the asking. When questions did arise, as happened seldom, my father showed lack of
interest, then claimed to have no memory of what was being
asked, and, finally, turned away with an impatient scorn,
showing an abrupt disdain for those who had asked him.

My father's repudiation of those early years, I realize now,
was highly disciplined and very nearly total; he had committed the years of his childhood and youth to an eternity of
death through silence. His desire, I suppose, was nothing
less than to eliminate history.

.

(I realize now that throughout my own boyhood, what my
father's silence and aloofness meant to me, as his son, was
this: When he was my age, when he was the way I am now,
my father had not existed.

In this way he successfully tyrannized me. It was as if he
were saying this of me: Unlike him, I alone remained visibly

encumbered with the embarrassing fact of my own awkward, inexperienced, and boyish existence.

He was free of such an encumbrance, while I was not.

I know this now not to have been true, that my father was a great liar.)

I

The record of my father's early years is largely absent, so I am forced to seek out traces of him among the records of other people and in the stories of those whose lives may have happened to touch on his.

There is, for example, the thin volume entitled *Harold Olaf Reiner: Christian Servant*, published in 1924 by the press of a small Lutheran college in Nebraska, written by a woman otherwise unknown to me named Elizabeth Hagen. I did not know that this book existed until after my father's death, when I found it stored among other of his personal belongings. Written obviously from close personal acquaintance, it is an adulatory book, filled with great praise of the life and achievements of my grandfather, and quite frequently overbearing. Still, within its pages are numerous small sightings, however indirect, of the nature of my father as a boy.

·

"In the spring of the year 1911, a call from his superiors caused the young Reverend Reiner upon short notice to leave his parish in northern Iowa and move with his family to the East, where the choice had fallen upon him to become the new pastor of a congregation (its own minister deceased) in Brooklyn, New York. By this time the small family was blessed already with two children, Harold and Signe, and the young Mrs. Reiner was pregnant, if not yet confined, with a third. They packed their household belongings, made the long journey by train, and settled in a four-story brownstone house off Fourth Avenue in the Bay Ridge section of Brooklyn, seven city blocks from the church. This pleasant but modest house was to remain the family's residence for the next fourteen years; it was to remain Dr. Reiner's only for the next twelve, until his premature and tragic death by pneumonia in January of 1923."

.

My father was raised in a pious and reverent family; yet in later life he was to become, however unsuccessfully, the rebellious, insolent, and scornful son of his own reverend father and of his nineteenth-century forebears. Knowing these things, I imagine adding a footnote to Elizabeth Hagen's text, in the formal manner of a scholar:

The eldest son was quite young at the time of his father's sudden death, having arrived at the age only of thirteen years. Yet it seems clear that the conflict he felt with his religious father was the force most singularly responsible for the early formation of his own personality and character. Even in his early years, as research in the family archives shows, the boy lived in a secret and intense repudiation of this father.

.

A citation revealing Elizabeth Hagen's text at the peak of its stylistic powers:

"Dr. Reiner was a man who brought with him into any room he entered the presence of generations past. In his authoritarian bearing, his stolidity, his sternness of demeanor—traits inherited from his own eminent and reverend father—he seemed to bring with him the sober dignities of history itself. To be castigated by him was to be castigated by the wise counsel of centuries. To be touched was to be touched by the pale hands of religious men lying in rows of tombs that extended backward into veils of mist. His power to humiliate those in error was vast, and his equally considerable power to praise was carefully guarded. It was inconceivable that he might ever falter in the belief that he was placed on earth to do good, to stand for right, to help his fellow man, and to express the thanksgiving and praise justly due a stern and charitable God.

"With his elevation in rank and his move to Brooklyn, the comforts of the well-ordered household improved. Some months before the birth of the third child (a second daughter, to be christened Hannah), a housekeeper was engaged for the purpose of helping with the large variety of household tasks confronting the young Mrs. Reiner, her duties not to exclude helping with the care of the children and with the cooking and serving of meals. She was given the small bedroom on the ground floor rear, whose narrow window opened onto the small back garden, where, on fair days, the children were set out on the grass to play."

.

(It became apparent quite early that the eldest son was to inherit his father's long limbs, high brow, and physical height. The paternal family resemblance in the child was striking. In his eyes could be seen a remarkable similarity to the father's, and a clear physical echo was to be perceived as well in the nose, facial structure, and the shape of the tall skull. The boy grew lean, and from an early time he was tall for his age. In his lips the shape of the father's mouth was refined and made more delicate, the upper lip especially possessing a fine and sensitive curvature that could more accurately be called beautiful than handsome and that presented to the observer a faint suggestion almost of the epicene. Throughout his early life and into young manhood he drew attention and was remarked upon for his physical beauty.

The sins of this child, especially as he approached the early years of adolescence, were: insolence, sullenness, vanity, pride, arrogance, irreverence, abuse of the flesh, and, on certain occasions, deceit.)

.

The atmosphere of the household:

The family lived in an atmosphere of Evangelical piety. One day the little boy came in from the farmyard, and his mother asked him whether he had seen the peacock. "I said yes, and the nurse said no, and my mother made me kneel down and beg God to forgive me for not speaking the truth."

—EMINENT VICTORIANS

.

My father's bedroom is on the top floor of the house, facing the street. It is a small room with one window. The bed is covered with a brown Boy Scout blanket tucked in tightly under the edges of the mattress so that the surface of the bed is firm and smooth.

On one wall hangs a Boy Scout canteen with a metal cap and a canvas carrying jacket. Near it hangs a painting that shows the ruins of a Roman temple against a turbulent purple and red sunset. Half of the columns of the temple remain standing; the others lie broken in drumlike segments on the earth. Reaching into the foreground, smaller pieces of broken marble are scattered in long grass. Commanding the center of the picture, a portion of the architrave remains erect.

A small table serves for my father's desk. On one corner is a pile of books, including a Latin primer and a book of world geography. Elsewhere on the surface of the desk are a Boy Scout jackknife, an English penny (the gift of an uncle returning from a European journey), and a polished chestnut with a string passed through it and then knotted so that the chestnut might be swung in circles. On the smooth bedcover lies an open book, face down. It is *The Young Carthaginian*, by G. A. Henty.

There is no one in the room. The window is opened wide; from time to time a soft breeze causes the thin white curtains to billow gently into the room, or to be pulled out in such a way that they might be visible to passersby in the street.

II

"In spite of the continually increasing burdens placed upon Dr. Reiner—his duties in the church and among the members of the congregation, his publishing and editing tasks, his chairmanship of the trustees' board at the Immigrants' Hospital, his new secretaryship of the Council—he managed always to keep a welcome place in his heart for his own family and home. Even in his frequent and sometimes extended absences from the head of the table (as in his journeys to the Middle West in receipt of his honorary degrees), the members of the family were assured of his spiritual presence, and in their prayers before the evening meal their desire for his well-being and their gratitude for his love were certain to be given expression. For this was, clearly, a harmonious household, held together by the bonds of Christianity and love. How inspiring it was for the present writer to be a visitor there and see the devoted Mrs. Reiner, with the help of the young housemaid Claire, cheerfully serving her four young children their breakfasts in the morning, packing their lunches, and seeing them off to school from the front steps of the house. On their return in the afternoon, they would more often than not be greeted by the smell of baking from the back kitchen, and after a treat of fresh bread with milk, or perhaps a pastry or cake, each of them would help in some variety of small household chore that was their particular allotment. After the evening meal came the time for schoolwork, for practicing musical instruments, or simply for finding a quiet corner and losing themselves for an hour or two in a book of their choosing. When all were fortunate enough for their father to be at home, it was not unusual for the family to gather together in the front parlor for the pleasure of hearing the master of the house read aloud. These were precious moments, of a peacefulness that might well symbolize the happiness of only the most blessed of families. The four children sitting on the carpet at his feet, their mother with a piece of needlework in a chair nearby, a fire burning quietly in the grate, Dr. Reiner would read aloud ancient folk tales from Norway, amusing chapters from certain of the English novelists, or, in the special seasons, passages from the Bible itself, chosen in keeping with the holy times of the year.

"His voice, as any know who may have had the good fortune to hear it, was quiet, expressive, and commanding. Familiar equally to his congregation as to his family, it was a voice formal yet comforting in its tone, and in its expression deep, resonant, and calm."

.

When he reached the age of twelve, my father was confirmed. He was required to say, standing before the gathered church: "I believe in God the Father Almighty, Maker of heaven and earth."

He was then asked: "What is meant by this Article?"

And he answered, skepticism writhing like a wounded snake deep inside him: "I believe that God has created me and all that exists; that He has given and still preserves to me my body and soul with all my limbs and senses, my reason and all the faculties of my mind, together with my raiment, food, home and family, and all my property; that He daily provides me abundantly with all the necessaries of life, protects me from all danger, and preserves me and guards me against all evil; all which He does out of pure, paternal, and divine goodness and mercy, without any merit or worthiness in me, for all which I am in duty bound to thank, praise, serve, and obey Him. This is most certainly true."

.

Of course there was no one to observe this rebellion inside my father; no one to interpret the symptoms of his gathering scorn for the church, for its liturgy, for his own father. My father's resentment remained from the beginning a secret known only to himself, nourished inwardly, resolutely without words.

.

Imagine a psychologist. Imagine a report made for his files: Harold Reiner is a precocious boy, intellectually gifted, above average in his ability to master his schoolwork in history, languages, mathematics, composition, the sciences. His being passed ahead, at twelve years of age, from the seventh to the ninth grade is a sure measure of this precocity. But his emotional growth is not equivalent. He is a remarkably handsome, even beautiful, youth. But his habitual sullenness, his subtle arrogance, and the myriad small ways (his tone of voice, his slowness to answer, the calculated self-consciousness of his physical bearing) with which he consistently expresses superiority and insolence in any situation where authority is imposed upon him can be signs only of a frustrated growth and a psychoemotional impaction of some intensity.

.

My father did this: He skipped school and spent the day at the neighborhood library reading *The Picture of Dorian Gray*. At this time he was twelve years old. The seriousness of the offense did not lie as greatly in the book he chose to read as it did in the deceitfulness of his action. The sin was the sin not of intellectual pride but of deceit.

Appropriate punishment was determined by his father to be confinement to his bedroom at all times, with the exception of school hours, for the duration of two weeks. He would in this way be removed from the bosom of the family even during mealtimes. Claire was to bring his meals to his room, where he would eat them, like a prisoner, alone at his desk. The single additional exception to this solitude was that his father, on the first and last nights of the penance, would climb the stairs, enter the room, kneel at the bedside, and pray at length for the soul of his eldest son.

III

"In 1917, when the United States entered the European
War, Dr. Reiner was made national director of the church's
Council for the Spiritual Well-Being of Members of the Army
and Navy. This was a position, in those years of hardship and
darkness, that placed even heavier demands upon his ener-
gies than before and required even greater sacrifice from his
family. It was necessary for him to travel frequently to the
national offices in Washington, D.C., and at certain times
during the length of the war he was unable, for as long as a
month at a time, to return home to his family and congregation.

"It is sobering to consider that it was the war itself, if in-
directly, that caused his death, he who labored so strenuously
to alleviate its hardships and suffering. Yet if he had not ex-
celled in co-ordinating the efforts of the synods in providing
ministry to the sailors and soldiers suffering abroad, his great
gift of administrative skill might well have gone unnoticed.
And in all likelihood, in the year but one following the end of
the war, he would not have been elected with almost unani-
mous support to the presidency itself of the National Council
of Synods. And had he not become president of that body,
at a time of grave international emergency, the burden of the
church's effort to extend relief to the masses of believers suffering in the aftermath of the European war would not have
fallen so squarely upon his own willing shoulders.

"It was this relief effort, representing for him almost four
years of labor and two arduous and extended journeys to the
suffering nations of Europe, that slowly undermined his robust constitution and rendered him unable to fight off the

disease of the lungs that, only twelve days after returning from his final journey, claimed nothing less than his life."

•

My father stands at the rail of the promenade looking out over the harbor toward the buildings of lower Manhattan. Near him are his mother, his two sisters Hannah and Signe, and his small brother Rolf.

It is a day of warm sunlight in the autumn of 1921. A gentle breeze comes off the water of the harbor, which is spotted in the distance with the white triangular sails of small boats. Closer in, two ferries pass one another slowly, one of them coming toward the city, the other moving away. Old men sit on the slatted benches along the promenade, warming themselves in the sunlight. Tables have been set up here and there, and games of checkers are being played. Young mothers and fathers push bonneted babies in prams.

The rail becomes more crowded as two airplanes can be heard flying down the river. They are frail, old-fashioned biplanes, strutted and wired, with exposed radial engines. The pilots' heads and goggled faces are visible in the open cockpits as they pass underneath the Brooklyn Bridge and fly only a few feet above the water along the length of the promenade. People in the crowd shout out greetings to them. The pilots wave their hands, gloved in black. Then they turn out toward the open harbor and gain altitude, flying wing to wing.

When they are high up against the blue sky, they turn suddenly outward from one another and roll over in midair. They dive downward at great speed, only to recover themselves above the surface of the water and climb again slowly to rejoin one another in the sky. Their engines buzz and drone in the distance.

The planes perform this trick and others like it for fifteen or twenty minutes. At one point they flutter downward, spinning slowly like kites with broken strings. They climb again, fly in loops, chase one another, dive and swoop. When the accident occurs, the crowd believes at first that it is another part of the show. The planes are very high up against the sky, rolling over one another. For a moment they seem to falter very slightly, as if their wings have touched, remained hooked together for a brief moment, then pulled apart. One of them falls away from the other and begins a steep dive, coming closer and closer to the water. The dive seems to take a long time, and, at the end, instead of pulling out, the plane plunges into the harbor with a modest, insignificant splash.

At first there is an instant of silence; then screams come from the length of the promenade and there is a new, sudden kind of pushing and movement in the crowd amid the noise. Meanwhile, the second plane descends from the sky in a long, gradual spiral. The sound of its engine is unnaturally loud, as if straining, and the plane continues descending slowly. At last, leveling out far over the harbor, it seems to have stabilized itself. It skims over the surface of the water for several moments. Then a wingtip catches the water, and, as if with great ease, the wing is torn off. The tail of the plane lifts upward, the fuselage lurches forward, remains standing briefly upright, then falls into the water with the cockpit underneath, and the sound of the engine is snuffed out.

·

Later still, suppose that an imaginary psychologist had composed a paper on the subject of my father for delivery before an assembly of his colleagues. Perhaps it would have sounded like this:

Indeed, these matters may be assumed to have been long since agreed upon and are perhaps beside the point here. It is a necessary commonplace in the development of any male child, consciously or subconsciously, to wish at some point for the death of its male parent; but it is considerably less common and indeed quite alarming for that wish to be accompanied early on, through the work of fate, by the actual occurrence of the willed event.

The depth of trauma caused by such an occurrence will depend upon a great number of variables; but it is clear that the degree and intensity of resentment felt previously by the child toward the dead parent must be the primary determinant of the depth of guilt and psychoemotional trauma to be sustained upon the sudden coming to pass, and at an early and formative age, of the darkly willed unspeakable.

In the case we are concerned with, this previous resentment was by all appearances deep, complex, and almost wholly unexpressed—owing to the formalized piety, the orderly habits, the reserved temperament of the family, and not least to the unfalteringly dominant and emotionally aloof position of the father.

Buried resentment in a situation such as this might be understood to make the potential death of the father an earnestly yearned-for event in view of the precocious child's own self-interest and dominant will to live in a sovereignty of his own. Yet the death of that father, however liberating it might prove to be in this one way, would necessarily mean at the same time the ripping away of the child's primal mirror, however imperfect or despised that may have been—the removal traumatically of that very instrument by which alone he could be enabled to arrive at a definition of himself: the removal, indeed, of his own mirror-image, with the very probable result of an intense and prolonged crisis in self-definition that might well last throughout a lifetime. Indeed, the physical death of the father might be expected to create in a child such as this a rigorous, knotted, and tightly embattled complex of contradictory emotions consisting most saliently of 1) exhilarating joy, 2) deeply paralyzing guilt, 3) violent rage, and 4) the terror, in a way not wholly subconscious, that he himself, in the death of the father, had also died.

.

In a letter to her husband, which reached him a month later in the city of Saratov, on the Volga, my grandmother referred to the "pitiful incident" of the airplanes and described it at considerable length for her husband, who could not otherwise have been expected easily to imagine it. She was deeply grieved, my grandmother explained, that what had begun as a pleasant family outing should have ended in disaster, and especially that fate should have required the children to be witnesses of so appalling a tragedy. That very evening (she wrote), gathered at the evening meal, the five of them prayed together, as a family, for the souls of the lost fliers.

It is from the single source of that letter, preserved by chance among other surviving family papers, that I know about this incident. My father never spoke of it to me, nor, so far as I have been able to discover, did he mention it to any other person during his adult life, not even to my mother in the three decades of their marriage. Like almost everything else from his early years, it was relegated by my father to silence, to the deep burial that he created through his passion-bound and unremitting wordlessness.

But from reading the letter I know with historical certainty that my father was there on that day; that he was standing on the promenade in the autumn sunlight with his mother, his two sisters, and his young brother. As for the rest, I can only imagine: that he may have been thinking of his absent father; that he was wishing secretly that the airplanes would fall. And I can only imagine the thrilled, excited depths of his awe and amazement as, standing in the warm sunlight at the iron rail, he saw the astonishing spectacle himself, his unspeakable desire come true: airplanes falling from the air. Frightened and amazed enough, indeed, never to mention it, throughout all of his life, to a living soul.

IV

"Again and again throughout eastern Europe [wrote Elizabeth Hagen], but most particularly inside Soviet Russia itself, Dr. Reiner was greeted by scenes confirming for him the calamity and the magnitude of the doom that had befallen not only the people themselves, but also their precious freedom of worship. In small Russian villages, their citizens suffering from famine, poverty, and disease, and beset further by new laws restricting even the uses of their own churches, the common people would congregate in open squares, kneeling in the sunlight on bare pavements as a means of expressing to him directly their gratitude for the shipments of grain and clothing sent by the organizations he represented, and their reverence and awe for a figure of the living faith the simple practice of which was now jeopardized and very nearly outlawed for them.

"These journeys were difficult for him in a degree hardly easy for us to imagine. He survived most of the time on subsistence rations no better than those the poorest peasants were provided to eat, believing it merely hypocritical that he should be privileged in any way above those whose needs he had come to serve. Repeatedly, he was escorted to small hovels or cellar rooms crowded with twenty or even thirty orphaned children, all kept alive in conditions of the most pitiable squalor. There were other signs as well of an ominous and oppressive kind to any who carried within him the will toward freedom and love. He was stopped at each border and in each city by the omnipresent secret police, who opened his luggage, read his private papers, even removed and searched the clothing he wore, showing no regard for the dignity of his person or for the political immunities of his religious mission. Again and again he came upon empty churches in even the smallest of parishes, their pastors having been tried and brutally imprisoned on the fabricated charges of having used their churches or the prestige of their faith to create counter-revolutionary forces against the powers of the new state.

"Amid such conditions as these, it becomes more easily understandable that Dr. Reiner was able with difficulty to set aside the natural repugnance he had always felt toward any form of personal idolization and to suffer stoically the idolatrous expressions of gratitude given him by the countless Russian villagers and peasants whom he visited. It became more and more frequently necessary for him to stand with forbearance in open marketplaces while the populations of whole villages filed past, kneeling one by one and, with the utterance of a brief prayer, kissing the toes of his shoes. He wrote of these overwhelming experiences in letters home to the small family awaiting his return in Brooklyn. 'It is in no way pleasant to speak of such extremities of the human spirit,' he wrote, 'but I have seen them with my own eyes and they are of the greatest importance. They are yet further and irrefutable proof that we must continue in our struggle to keep even the dimmest light shining. We must be unflagging and tireless in our efforts to alleviate and bring to an end this suffering of our fellow believers under the mailed fist of an enemy so implacably evil, and in the horrifying face of adversities so appalling as these.'"

.

Dressed in a suit and necktie, my father stood with others his own age in the church in Brooklyn while his reverend father—by now eminent, famous, world-traveled—catechized them. He singled out his own son and asked him: *"What does God declare concerning these commandments?"*

Before row upon row of the congregation gathered as witness to the ritual, my father answered, each word a blasphemy flying out to touch the walls of the church: "He says: I the Lord thy God am a jealous God, visiting the iniquity of the fathers upon the children unto the third and fourth generations of them that hate Me . . ."

.

His youthful torment and pride, his isolation, his fear and rage: forty years later, living with my father when I was growing up in a farmhouse on the plains of Minnesota, I felt the presence of these forces as shadows over my own life, was touched by them as surely as if they had been physical things, even though never spoken of, entombed in silence.

V

My grandfather returned from Europe for the last time on January 15th, 1923, twelve days before his death. The evening of his return is described by Elizabeth Hagen, who was included in the gathering, it seems, as an intimate guest of the family:

"After dinner, the family and those few especially close friends who had been chosen to share in the special intimacy of Dr. Reiner's first evening at home after his long journey rose from the table and gathered in the front parlor. A fire burned in the grate, warming the room and drawing the members of the company to take seats near it. Coffee was poured and served to the guests by the two young daughters, Hannah and Signe, although not before they had first served their father, one of them holding for him the tray with cup and saucer, the other offering sugar and milk.

"He had brought homecoming gifts; even in the prolonged extremities of his journey, he had not forgotten his family. All eyes watched as he carefully laid back small folds of velvet and exposed a small but exquisitely cut Russian diamond, which, with a pleasure that could not be concealed, he offered to his wife, the gem still resting on its velvet cushion. For each of the children as well, he had brought a carefully chosen gift. For Rolf, the youngest, there was a small toy automobile with a Swiss clockwork motor. For the two girls there were a doll made of Venetian china and a small cut-glass bottle of French scent. For the eldest son, Harold, already the most literary of the children, he had brought an English first edition, handsomely bound in leather, of Robert Louis Stevenson's romantic novel *The Master of Ballantrae*.

"The exhausting demands made upon him by his missions abroad were evident in the changes that now had been brought about in his physical appearance. He was dramatically thinner than he had been at the start of his last journey, his color was poor, and darkened areas were clearly evident under his eyes, giving the suggestion of deep fatigue. Although she gave no sign of it in front of the children, his wife was alarmed to see the faint tremor of his hand as he raised a cup to his lips. It was another mark of his selflessness and dedication to his calling that he would not tolerate, even on this notable occasion, any expressions of concern about the state of his health. Leaning forward in his chair to cover for a moment his wife's hands with both of his own, he dismissed the topic with a gentle peremptoriness by asserting simply that his health was strong, and reminding us all once again that God's divine protection was yet stronger.

"In spite of the great suffering he had so recently both witnessed and endured, he entertained us pleasantly—especially so long as the children remained part of the company—with anecdotes and entertaining descriptions from his journeys, including the dramatic adventure of a dangerous and storm-tossed home-crossing, and a detailed description of the depths of his emotional response, two weeks before that return voyage, at finding himself, one day near sundown, standing at the center of the majestic ruins of the great Roman Colosseum, on that precise and hallowed round of earth where almost two thousand years before the early Christians had been placed into martyrdom.

"Only after the four children had been excused from the company and had gone upstairs to their beds did he allow himself, at first with reluctance and then with increasing warmth, to speak openly of the grim realities of neglect, loss, and spiritual degradation that he had lived with on the most intimate of terms for the past half-year. The human suffering he had witnessed was great. Faint color rose to his pale

cheeks as he went on, speaking of the tyranny and godless-
ness, the awesome depravity, the murder of faith itself that
he knew to be pressing with cold savagery and gathering
strength against our world from the east.

"With deep commitment and a quiet, controlled passion,
he spoke at length to his small group of spellbound listeners.
Only after a considerable time did his voice come to a stop.
By then it was late in the evening, and for several long moments, struck with wonder and awe by what we had heard,
the rest of the company remained wordless. In the hush that
ensued, broken only by the somber ticking of the hallway
clock, the still house around us seemed to have become filled
with a suggestive immanence. Almost like an omen, the fire
collapsed on the grate with a quiet rustling of ash as the
returned missionary gazed somberly into it. No word was
spoken to break the ineffable spell of that moment. Never,
I believe, have I sensed such moral power and vital faith to
reside within one man as I sensed at that moment to reside
within him. Surely he was a devoted servant of our Lord."

VI

The father and son kneel together beside the boy's bed in
the top floor of the house. The occasion that brings them into
this posture together is the termination of the boy's two-week
penance of solitude in his room.

Their heads are bowed, their hands are folded on the
smooth blanket, and the father prays at great length. The
effect of this prayer, particularly in its opening and conclud-
ing stages, is to create in the young son a sense of worthless-
ness, shame, dependence, and humiliation. His father, pray-

ing with his eyes closed, begs God first for the forgiveness of those sins the boy is known already to have committed. He describes these sins. He goes on to pray for the prevention of those sins the boy has not yet committed but which he shows a predilection for committing. The father cites these sins also, along with the weaknesses and flaws in the boy's character that make the occurrence of them seem most likely. Taken together, the offenses are numerous. To the boy's imagination, particularly if privately he feels already misunderstood, emotionally excluded, and unfairly prejudged, they may well seem vast in number and very possibly overwhelming. Coming from his father's lips, slow word by slow word, in a quiet and unemotional monotone, they may seem to gather slowly like irrievable citations to an endless damnation, to accumulate first

the question of humility, Wilde is a writer of great intellectual wit and immense popularity. But it is true also that he possesses not a shred of living faith and that he is grievously prideful of this fact. The garment of his faith is threadbare and rent, and therefore how can he teach? Yet even disregarding this question, there is another requirement, and that is a moral one. Clear dangers are created by Wilde's failure to meet it. But not even this, as not pertaining directly to ourselves, is our crucial point. Our crucial point is that what you have done, the act itself, regardless of its end, is sinful and deceitful. As also are those similar things that you have done previously and kept secret to yourself. And those things that you may have desired to do but have not yet done. These too are sins, a fact which is a profound truth of great and extreme importance and one that we must understand. In our hidden desires, our

                           huge wide back, rounded like a black bear's. Big sloping shoulders. My father is ponderous, he is growing fatter. The flesh of his big arms straining against the black cloth. Even at the swollen back of his neck, when I peer sideways to look while he is praying, where the stiffened collar presses deeply into

                           gray cobwebby shadows, like the masses of tentworms in the walnut trees at his uncle Gunnar's farm in the Catskills, gathering in the upper corners of the room, then descending as they fill the space of the room and press downward, like something that could suffocate you, toward the surface of the bed with its smooth brown

                           responsibility. We do not have excuses. We do not have exemptions. The time will come when we do not have second chances. Each of us is unworthy. Each of us contains sinfulness within him, as a diseased man who may seem hale and well carries within his body unseen corruption. It is because of this corruption that God has justly prepared for us everlasting fire. The burning lake is a damnation whose horrors we cannot begin to conceive. To hold our finger in the flame of a candle is not a millionth part of what we must imagine in order to begin to know what an eternity in hell would mean to the damned soul. And yet we are not lost to this terrible condemnation. In His divine and supreme charity, God has given to each of us the most priceless of gifts, having bequeathed upon each sinner

                              fingers thick and padded, the skin white like something that is never in the sun. The thickets of black bristles growing in tangles on their backs, like the hair of miniature beasts. Think: the pigs' backs in the barnyard at Uncle Gunnar's, mottled pink and black, their stiff bristles

           conceived by the Holy Ghost, Born of the Virgin Mary; Suffered under Pontius Pilate, was crucified, dead and buried; He descended into hell; The third day He rose again from the dead; He ascended into heaven, And sitteth on the right hand of God the Father Almighty; from thence He shall come

           by train, at the end of June when school is out, and then Gunnar meets us with the wagon drawn by slow old Hattie. As always, we have come with lumps of sugar for Hattie in our pockets, her lips curling to take them up from the palms of our hands, the hot wet air snorting softly from her huge nostrils. My mother climbs up and rides on the wooden seat with Gunnar, the rest of us, the children, sitting on pieces of luggage in back. On the first day of the vacation there is always the excitement of the animals, Hannah and Signe and

Rolf holding the new lambs, counting how many are in the litters of pigs, naming kittens for the summer, romping on the lawn with Ganges, and before dinner we all try our hand at drawing milk from the two cows, until Gunnar, laughing at us, takes the stool and milks them himself, the thin streams piercing with a hollow sound into the bottom of the empty bucket and then the warm white foam building up. At dinner Sonja brings in the cold milk from the day before in a brown pitcher with drops of water on its smooth sides, and the fresh bread comes under a warm checkered napkin, and Gunnar winks every time at little Hannah and says he's certain God doesn't want our food to get cold, and Hannah doesn't know whether it's safe to laugh or not, so she peeks sideways at my mother, who is already looking down at her own folded hands, and so then Gunnar says a short prayer, as often as not in Norwegian, and it's hardly begun before it's over. Gunnar is the one who gave me a cigarette for the first time, resting together in the shade of one of the haystacks, then helped me find wild mint beside the lane on the way back to the house to chew and hide the smell. The other time when he tousled my head in the sun on the lawn when we were leaving at the end of August and told everyone he was going to keep me through the winter since he needed good helpers, having no children of his own, and he hooked his arm around my neck and pulled me toward him, his bare arm warm and firm, the golden hair on it soft like fur, and the side of his chest like a great warm barrel, and then the sound of his easy laughter. In my room with Rolf at night there is no screen on the window, and the window stays open all through the night, cool air coming in, and in the morning there is the pure sunlight and cool sweet air and the grand sight of the valley stretching off as far as you can see, the big sides of the mountains sloping down into it, meadow and forest and shadow with different shades of green, and then the amber and gold and brown patchwork of the fields in the valleys, some of them Gunnar's, and other houses nestled into the sides of the valley in the distance, woodsmoke curling out of their kitchen chimneys. I believe I would stay there forever, alone with just Gunnar and Sonja, even through the deep winters when the snow drifts up to the eaves and you can't get out of the house, waiting for the warm thaws and the coming of spring and the meadows filled with wildflowers if I were

a lost and condemned creature, secured and delivered me from all sins, from death, and from the power of the devil, not with silver and gold, but with His holy and precious blood, in order that I might be His, live under Him in His kingdom, and serve Him in everlasting righteousness, innocence, and blessedness, even

hiking boots with wool socks, my Scout shorts, and the shirt with big front pockets. Nothing else. I walk with a knobbed mountain stick Gunnar helped me cut from a cherrywood, and in one pocket I have my knife, in another my compass, and on my back my canteen and the small canvas pack with the three sandwiches Sonja made for me and one early apple and Gunnar's small pair of binoculars that he let me take along. Telling me exactly how to go, to stay on the southeast slope and just keep climbing, judge by the sun and by landmarks and by the compass if I need it, and once I got to the top I would be able to see three ranges farther to the west, a distant opening out, thirty miles perhaps, so long as the day was clear enough and I had the binoculars to look through. Sonja gave me breakfast before the others were awake, the house quiet and strangely hushed, before the sun had even slanted down yet into the valley, and when I set out, Ganges came around the corner of the house and leaped all over me and wanted to follow along, except that Gunnar, standing then on the edge of the porch, called him back and made him sit, and then the two of them stood there watching while I

reflect on your condition, according to the Ten Commandments, namely: Whether you are a father or mother, a son or daughter, a master or mistress, a manservant or maidservant—whether you have been disobedient, unfaithful, slothful—whether you have injured anyone by words or actions—whether you have stolen, neglected, or wasted aught, or

thinking of the mountain under me, the vastness and enormity of it, heavy, durable, solid, almost like something alive, and I had already planned my resting times, the first after one hour, then another after the second hour, and so on, and I should be at the top by eleven o'clock, time enough for two hours on the peak before starting down. But just after my first rest I heard something and paused, waited to hear it again, a call coming through the warming air. Far down the grassy slope some-

thing moved in the sunlight, Ganges bounding through the
long grass, and, still farther down, the tiny figure of Gunnar,
standing with his hands cupped to his mouth, hallooing to
me up the sun-drenched flank of the mountain, the warmth
of it, bees starting to gather nectar from the flowers, and then
the dry swish of the tall grass as I turned and started down
again toward

                our flocks gathered under this roof to pray in
a time of fear and great loss, when evil occasions and history's darkening march require a

                           telegram has come from my
father, Gunnar said; my mother was packing already for the
afternoon train back to the city, in a very great hurry, all
of us were to go back with her. A special service next day
at the church, and then the day after that my father was
to take passage on

             Gunnar said perhaps next summer

                                 but I
thought to myself, no, my father will find some way to destroy
it again, the way he destroys all my

                        protection be sought
through prayer for the journeys of Christ's servants in the

time of our greatest need, when the sails of our vessels are torn and their masts are broken

together on the wagon seat, Gunnar and me, Hattie pulling us along quietly, the spoked wheels turning slowly in the dust of the lane, sunlight warm and steady across our shoulders. Ganges loping playfully behind us, snapping at white butterflies that rise up out of the grass, and Gunnar's cheerful laughter, the two of us chewing mint leaves, and Gunnar puts his arm around my shoulders for a moment, laughing lightly, amused by the memory, and asks me if I remember the time when he

let us then for these reasons kneel here, and let us pray together; let us open ourselves up and accept the light of the Lord; let us not be ashamed to recognize our degradation and debasement, the great evil and vile selfishness of our desires, the depravity of the flesh within which we live, and let us admit to one another openly the unworthy corruption of our souls and hearts; let us then bow our heads; let us clasp our hands together; let us humble ourselves before our Creator, and let us in our extreme unworthiness and in the extremity of our need ask the blessed forgiveness and the eternal guidance of our God, and of His Son, Jesus Christ, our Lord

I hate my father, I wish he were dead.

VII

"After his return from Europe, Dr. Reiner set aside no time for much needed rest, but plunged directly into his work, spending with his family only what little segments of the day he was able to pry free for himself. The urgency of the task remained great, and after only four days with his family and congregation in Brooklyn, he traveled to the city of Buffalo to preside over the annual meeting of the National Council, where it was essential that he communicate once again to the leaders of the synods not only the appalling extent of suffering that persisted in the war-ravaged countries, but also the grimly intensifying threat to the very existence of the church as he had personally witnessed it. During the conference, he was known to be suffering from a chest cold, but after the second day this seemed to improve, and he complained only of infrequent chills and a difficulty in keeping warm, symptoms to which he gave insufficient regard, attributing them merely to the January weather, which at that time was especially piercing and damp.

"He traveled from Buffalo to Cleveland, where a full schedule of services had been planned in the city's churches, he himself scheduled to deliver no fewer than four guest sermons on the vital importance of the continuing relief appeal. He was accompanied to Cleveland by Dr. Sogn, with whom on Sunday evening he shared dinner and with whom the next morning he breakfasted, remaining in conference with him and other church leaders until shortly past noon. Dr. Sogn commented that at dinner on Sunday evening Dr. Reiner did appear fatigued by his unremitting schedule, but that the symptoms of his illness seemed largely to have disappeared

and that Dr. Reiner impressed him then just as he had so
many times in previous years as being a man of great strength
and in the prime of life, possessing the full vigor of his mind,
body, and spirit.

"The next morning, after a full night's rest, his fatigue
seemed alleviated, and the breakfast conference was said
to have been energetic and productive. No further thought
was given to the question of Dr. Reiner's health. But during
the night he was visited by a serious relapse, and on Tuesday morning he begged of Dr. Sogn that he felt unable just
then to proceed on to Pittsburgh as had been planned. With
regret, he suggested a delay. Not yet greatly alarmed, Dr.
Sogn sent telegrams on to Pittsburgh and to the family in
Brooklyn with information as to what had occurred and as to
the change in schedule.

"The situation, however, failed to improve, and in fact it
worsened rapidly. Late Wednesday night the doctors insisted
that the patient be admitted to Calvary Hospital, and some
hours later a diagnosis of pneumonia was formally announced.
In the late hours of Wednesday night the alarm was sent out
to all quarters. Most important, Dr. Sogn directed a telegram to the house in Brooklyn, informing Mrs. Reiner of the
gravity of the situation and urging her with all possible speed
to come to her husband's side. Shortly before dawn on Thursday, she left the city by train and arrived in Cleveland at six
o'clock that evening. In this way, through God's grace, she
was able to be with her beloved husband, at his bedside, for
the final twelve hours of his life.

"He struggled valiantly, but in his weakened condition following his European journeys the onslaught of the disease
was overpowering. It seemed apparent to those with him that
in the final hours he resigned himself to the inevitable, no

longer questioning for what reasons beyond mortal understanding his lifelong work had been willed suddenly to an
end. He felt with deep confidence that he was at one with his
God, and this knowledge enabled him to die placidly and in
peace, holding, through the ultimate moment and the end of
his earthly life, the hand of his beloved and devoted wife.

"His widow accompanied the body on its journey back to
the city, and from the station she accompanied it to its temporary resting place inside the church of which until so recently
her husband had been the spiritual head. By this time she had
been absent from her children for very nearly three full days.
Escorted to her home, she met them at the doorway, but
spoke no word until all of them, in silence, had taken their
places with her around the dining room table and joined their
hands together over its polished surface. Only then did she
speak, quietly but with great firmness and strength, holding
back the tears of grief that in spite of her great faith pressed
upon her grievously from within. The Lord, she told her children, had taken their father from this earthly life. But he was
with them still; he was in their very presence: indeed, she
knew with the very certainty of her faith itself that he would
never leave any one of them, but that he would cling to the
essence of their souls forever; that his undying spirit would
remain with each one of them, living within them, throughout the rest of their lives."

Epilogue

1. When did my father arrive in West Tree, Minnesota?

My father arrived in West Tree, Minnesota, at three-seven-
teen on the afternoon of Saturday, June 27th, 1925. When
the train pulled into the station, he was the first to step down

onto the red brick platform. He turned his head first one way, toward the front of the train, then the other, toward the rear, seeming after this to pause for a brief moment before making any further decision. He then turned and held up his hand for the four other passengers who were to get off the train. These were his mother, dressed in black with a veil drawn over her face; his eleven-year-old brother, wearing tweed knickers; and his two younger sisters, thirteen and fifteen years old.

My father himself had reached the age of sixteen. Because of the tragedy that had befallen them two years earlier, he was now the eldest male in the family. In the somewhat heady awareness of his privilege and responsibility, he was not above making the younger members of the family feel their new subservience to him, and they were able to feel even less than before that he was always to be trusted. In his manner and bearing there had appeared a new level of insolence which only now they were learning to live with, primarily by leaving him alone, by avoiding situations in which he could make most telling effect of his scorn, by no longer demanding the normally expected small courtesies of him, and, insofar as possible, by avoiding dependence upon him for the return of favors.

On an upper arm of each of the four children, visible in the steady June sunlight as they stepped off the train, was a discreet band of black cloth.

2. Where had my father and his family traveled from?

My father and his family had embarked upon their journey from the front steps of a brownstone townhouse off Fourth Avenue in the Bay Ridge section of Brooklyn, New York, a location, when the breeze came from the right quarter, within reach of the scent of the open sea. A cab, arranged for by the church, had taken them across the Brooklyn Bridge and uptown through the crowded streets of lower Manhattan to Grand Central Terminal. The air in the city was fresh with the smells of an early summer morning. Sea gulls wheeled in graceful spirals over the river. Sidewalks were hosed with water, and a pleasant coolness lingered in the shadows of the tall buildings in midtown. At Grand Central they boarded an overnight train for Chicago. In Chicago the next day, they changed to a train bound for Minneapolis, the Dakotas, Montana, Idaho, and the Pacific Northwest. It was from this train that they disembarked, in the sun-filled afternoon of June 27th, 1925, on the red brick platform of the station in West Tree, Minnesota.

3. What did my father and his family do immediately upon their arrival in West Tree, Minnesota?

For some moments after the train pulled out, they stood on the platform, surrounded by their numerous pieces of luggage, looking around them at their new surroundings. The day was remarkably quiet. Through an open window of the station building could be heard, on the soft air, the clicking of the station master's telegraph. From somewhere in the foliage of green trees on the far side of the tracks a bird began to sing. A cab appeared, turned in from the street, and drove slowly into the station lot. It came to a stop near where the family was standing. My father stepped over to the cab. Speaking consciously with a trace of Brooklyn accent in his voice, he arranged with the driver to convey the family to the house that awaited them in the town. He then stood by in the sunlight and watched with a certain insolent and detached interest—his hands resting comfortably in the pockets of his pleated trousers, his head cocked slightly to one side as if with a faint sense of wry bemusement and drollery—as the driver carried the pieces of heavy luggage from the red brick platform and, one by one, hoisted them up to the rack on top of the cab.

4. What, during his journey into the heart of the continent, had my father seen from the windows of the train?

He had seen the remarkable and exhilarating absence of his father, translated into the openness, freedom, and grandeur of the country. Crystalline sunlight. A high vault of blue sky. Wide fields of yellowing grain and green pastureland reaching to a distant range of hills veiled in blue haze. A wide river with barges moving slowly on its breeze-rippled surface. A team of dappled farm horses pulling a loaded wagon over a wooden bridge on a road below the train. Important to him in the experience of this westward travel were the scents that he breathed. The swift movement of the inland-bound train appealed to him most intensely as a metaphor of flight or of escape to freedom, and his pleasure was greatest when he stood in the open passageways between cars and leaned outward so the wind buffeted against his face. In this way he breathed in great volumes of fresh air fragrant with the odor of warm sunlight on recently dampened earth, the sweet dry scent of ripening grain, the smells of clover or fields of mown hay, the scent of coal smoke from the engine of the train itself, or the tang of wood burning in stoves, caught for a moment while passing through small, yellow-windowed towns near nightfall, then snatched away by the speed of the train as it moved on, flying through the cooling air into gathering darkness ahead.

THREE

(1925–1926)

I

She is selling tickets one evening at her father's theater. The year is 1925, the date September 6th. A warm evening breeze moves gently from the southwest, bringing with it the smells of the prairie and drying grasses, the warm scents of the end of summer.

A short time before the first movie begins, the evening grows dark enough so that the lights of the marquee are switched on. Lights are turned on also inside the glass-enclosed booth where the young woman sits on a small raised chair, selling tickets. She speaks to customers through the louvers of a circular brass fixture fitted into the glass. Some of the customers, familiar with her, exchange greetings and offer pleasantries. Others say nothing except to indicate the number of tickets they wish to buy.

The lighting inside the booth makes it seem almost as if the young woman herself is on display, like a painting or statue carefully highlighted in a museum. She wears lipstick, and the lashes of her eyes are darkened. Her black hair is cropped fashionably short and is brushed forward to surround her face like an oval frame, creating a vivid contrast to the milky whiteness of her skin.

After the first feature has begun, one or two stragglers request tickets and then disappear hurriedly through the open doors of the theater. Having sold them their tickets, the young woman sits for a time without seeming to move. Then she reaches down and brings up a book, which she lays open on the ticket ledge in front of her. It is a school reader in third-year French. She begins to read the opening pages of *Le Malade imaginaire*.

She looks up from the book when a tall young man comes into the circle of light under the marquee. Moving with a graceful absence of hurry, he comes to the ticket window and, saying nothing, places two coins on the ledge. The young woman slides his ticket out toward him, and she looks up into his eyes as she does so, but he turns away, and she is uncertain whether he has exchanged the look or not. She has never seen this young man before, and she continues to watch him—the back of his light-colored coat, the self-possessed carriage of his tall body—as he steps slowly into the theater and, hardly so much as looking about him, walks casually toward the closed doors of the auditorium.

II

She is attractive and has often been told so, inheriting her beauty from her parents, of whom she is an only child, yet she is neither vain about her appearance nor supercilious in her manner. She dresses carefully and is aware of being in fashion, yet clothing is not of dominating importance to her, and she is content frequently to wear garments that have grown older than most of her more frivolous classmates would willingly permit. She is intelligent and stands near the head of her class, yet she is neither cynical about the value of her studies nor arrogant about her achievements. Although she is not intellectually adventuresome or temperamentally a recluse, she does read more widely than her classmates, yet she remains undemonstrative about her knowledge, as though her reading were the result as much of passivity or aimlessness as of an active interest. She is not a member of any social clique, formal or informal. The number of her close friends is small, and with these she is unpresuming, polite, and affectionate, but neither intimate nor especially confiding. She is envied and admired for her beauty, but her more aggressive competitors take satisfaction in her lack of assertiveness and frivolity, believing that the absence of these traits, along with her air of slight reserve, will cause the interest of the more desirable young men to turn to others before turning to her. In general, this belief has proven to be true. She has gone with young men on hayrides, to dances and social evenings at school or on rare occasions elsewhere, but generally the young men have felt uncomfortable with her and have found conversation strained, with the result that she has seldom gone out with any of them more than once or twice. She is not isolated and she is not disliked, but her character and the peculiarities of her unnaturally mature temperament seem to place her more on the periphery than at the center of the society of her classmates and of those around her. She is observed, taken account of, and frequently admired, but no one has found a way of coming close enough to her to know her well or to bring her intimately into their own lives.

III

August 28th, 1926. From the window of his upstairs bedroom, Harold Reiner watches his two sisters taking turns
pushing one another on the swing at the far end of the back
yard. They are some distance away: the yard extends three
lots into the block, sheltered along its borders by the high
limbs of elm trees and the spreading branches of grown
maples. But from the window of his room the girls are never-
theless visible, and from time to time in the stillness of the
afternoon Reiner can hear their voices. They wear white
dresses that billow on the air behind them as they swing.
Dappled sunlight, penetrating through green leaves, moves
across their bodies as they move.

Harold Reiner is quite entirely separated from this gaiety
and movement. In his room, his feet rest on the desk that
faces the open window, and he leans back in his chair so
that only its two back legs are touching the floor. The desk
is cluttered with papers and books. On one corner are piled
a novel by Rölvaag, a volume of four plays by Ibsen, another
of Shaw, three copies of a college newspaper, and Wyndham
Lewis's *Tarr*. Reiner has lit a cigarette. Its smoke rises slowly
toward the ceiling from his poised hand as he gazes out the
window at his sisters.

His mother is at work in the kitchen below his room. Now
and then he hears the clatter of silverware or the sound of
pieces of crockery being placed one against the other. There
is to be a picnic lunch at the table in the back yard. Soon
his aunts Marie and Lutie Reiner, sisters of his recently dead
father, will arrive, walking up to the front door of the house

like formal visitors, wearing their wide-brimmed sun hats and long dresses.

Reiner continues gazing out the open window. He does not read, or write anything, or move. His sisters leave the swing and walk together, side by side in their white dresses, toward the back door of the house. He hears them come inside, and he is not surprised when some moments later his young brother Rolf climbs the stairs and appears at the open door of the room. For a moment Rolf is silent. Then he says, "Mother told me you're to come down and help the others of us get things ready."

Reiner turns his head to look at his brother where he stands in the door, wearing baggy shorts and a long-sleeved shirt. Then, as if the energy required to receive this image of the insignificant boy has not been worth the reward, he allows his gaze to return to the window. In his movement, he conveys an air of exhaustion.

"Did she so indeed?" he asks. The words are delivered with an unspeakably weary tone that seems aimed in about equal degrees of scorn at the messenger and at the message. "Perhaps I'll come down later. Meanwhile I'll stay where I am, thank you. I've got work to do. I'm going to see Eva tonight and won't be home. Tell people I don't want to be disturbed."

For a moment Rolf is silent, uncertain, as usual, how to respond to the imperious manner of his older sibling. He does not move, but stands in the doorway looking at his brother. As he stands there, studying what he sees, he seems scarcely to be breathing.

"Mother says you shouldn't smoke," he says.

Reiner leans forward and snubs his cigarette in the ashtray on his desk. "Do me the favor of telling Mother," he says to Rolf, still without looking at him, "that I am smoking a cigarette. Tell her also that I am about to smoke another. As for the rest, please stop occupying my otherwise perfectly serviceable doorway."

IV

September 11th, 1925. He emerged from the door of the tobacco shop on the main street of the town and saw her at the corner, waiting to cross. Seizing the moment, he stepped out of the doorway and took his place beside her. She looked up at him, and, seeing that it was the young man who had bought a ticket from her at the theater five days earlier, she smiled very slightly by way of greeting. He was intensely aware of the darkness of her eyes as she looked at him, and of the shape of her lips as she smiled. Without returning the smile, and without other introduction, he said coolly, gazing ahead into the distance as they stepped off the curb together: "I saw you were reading Molière the other night. That was certainly a surprise. I didn't know they could read French, way out here in the backwaters."

V

Those were my parents; that is how they met; that was the beginning of their courtship.

The street they crossed was paved with oiled wooden blocks. After crossing this street, they strolled to the river, walked onto the bridge, and, halfway across, they paused.

There they stood in the warm sunlight of the September afternoon, the river flowing beneath them, and talked for some time. My father leaned casually with his body against the rail. He lit a cigarette. A soft breeze arose now and then, bringing with it the redolent scent of autumn. It touched my mother's hair, and the cautious, pleased smile of her upturned face.

FOUR
(1933–1938)

Although she presented with some success an outward impression of stylish self-confidence, social independence, and a certain bohemian disdain for the less significant aspects of moral conformity, she was not a rebellious creature. More to the truth, she was a woman whose life was governed by fear as much as it ever could be by the apparent independence of her temperament. The many fears she possessed were both small and great, rooted predominantly in her childhood, and wide ranging in their variety. She feared disorder, violence of any kind (the result, perhaps, of her parents' excessive fighting when she was young), and the callousness of feeling that permitted or caused abuse of weakness by strength. She feared all forms of personal danger and the physical suffering (more in others than in herself, and more in children than in adults) that comes from injury to the flesh. She feared horses and to a lesser extent all large domesticated animals (especially if horned or hooved), unleashed dogs unless well known to her, and, in suspicion of their carrying diseases that might turn them vicious and poisonous, squirrels, skunks, foxes, all rodents, and bats. She feared lakes, ponds, and rivers, or any places, including bathtubs, where death by drowning could occur. She feared automobiles, cliffs, heights, ladders, airplanes, and high speeds. She feared the silent and lethal powers of electricity, and she feared pieces of exposed machinery in which any part of the body or clothing might be caught. She feared ice skates, sled runners, roller skates, and bicycles, broken glass, knives, ice picks, the lids of tin cans, household astringents and acids, communicable diseases, and all the kinds of poisoning conveyable through tainted, infected, or contaminated food. In dread of choking, she was frightened of the effect, especially on children, of popcorn, peanuts, hard candy, the pits of small fruits, olives, and fish bones. She feared pencils and sharp sticks, barbed wire, slingshots, metal shavings, and all materials of potential hazard to the eyes. More abstractly, she feared the coming of war and the disharmony of nations. She feared high winds, lightning, burglars, trespassers, and loud or sharp noises. From early childhood she had been afraid of brandished weapons, but in particular she was frightened of firearms and guns. When she became married (in the year 1933), she married for love, but also for protection.

As with many in their youth (but even more so with those more fortunate), time did not seem to press upon them, seemed almost not to be passing at all, did not appear before them, as it does before so many of us, as a relentless measurement of narrowing chances and diminishing opportunity. They lived together during these years within the charmed period of an Edenic and suspended moment. It seems evident that good luck alone—even in a time of general hardship—can be credited only partly with their possession of this happiness. Their devotion to one another, the perfection, balance, and harmony of their match, the serving of each of them as an enriching complement to the other—these are the things responsible most clearly for the attainment of this special quality in their lives.

There are photographs of them in the first year of their marriage: quiet summer afternoons at home with friends. In one of them, they stand together in backyard sunlight beside a rosebush, a glimpse behind them of white picket fence. (Not seen: the scent of grass, the warmth of sunlight on flesh, summer quietness, the sound of voices laughing lightly in quiet air.) The two of them are debonair, casual. He stands with one arm around her shoulders, his free hand resting loosely in his trouser pocket. She looks adoringly up at his face. He gazes at the camera, his tall head cocked slightly to one side, an expression of light, satisfied, controlled and slightly ironic amusement on his face, as though he is listening with pleasure to the laughter of others at a small joke he has made.

He studied carefully and at the same time he romanticized intensely the life around him, making of it, by a process of extremely careful selection, something other than in its wholeness it really was. His was a major, sustained, and perhaps a compulsive effort of romantic transfiguration. In the photographs (and to a lesser extent in the writings) of this period, he accumulated slowly and with great diligence an acceptable—that is to say, a safe, poised, stable and unchanging—definition of the world around him; and, in so doing, since he stood at the center of this world as perceived and recorded through the lens of his own eye, he arrived at an equivalent definition of himself, becoming in this process, as certainly he must in some sense have been aware, both creator and created. It might be said that he became a maker of many small mirrors.

She in ankle-length housedresses made of thin print material, belted at the waist, sometimes sleeveless, more often fitting tightly on the upper arm with the sleeves pleated and flared at the shoulders. He in loose pleated trousers, cuffed, worn extremely high at the narrow waist, fitted with wide leather belts. White cotton shirts with the collars unbuttoned and open, sleeves rolled up. Sometimes woolen tweed jackets which, through use, have grown shapeless and comfortable, often with leather patches at the elbows. In imitation of certain figures from the screen, he cultivates a mustache, tasteful, masculine, carefully trimmed.

She loved him for those qualities that in the later, desperate years, when time had defeated him, were to fester, rigidify, and paralyze him in the chill fury that would make him hostile, tyrannical, unloveable and cruel. She loved him for his stability, his calm energy, his insolently confident pride; she loved him for his kindness, his solicitude, his care and protectiveness; she loved him for the severities of his conscience, his seriousness, and his light, biting humor; she loved him for his reserved mysteriousness and aloofness, his love of beauty, and for the sense, not closely examined but shared by them both as their greatest and most intimate secret, that within him lay the promise for greatness.

Motes visible in a thick shaft of sunlight falling through a front window, touching her coat hanging in the empty vestibule. Houseplants on a sill, beside them a small watering can with a slender, arched spout. A windowpane seen from inside, streaked with raindrops, the vague image of a bare tree outside. Rosebuds seen through an open kitchen window. Two white bottles of milk standing on the front doorsill, beaded with moisture. Interior of an upstairs bedroom, the sheets rumpled, a corner trailing to the floor, the window open wide, sunlight on thick foliage just outside. (The room, otherwise, is empty, save for a slender rocking chair in one corner, and, draped over it, a woman's garment.)

He was drawn to the camera as the best means by which to achieve his purpose because of the ease with which he could control its process of selection, because of the rewarding muteness, passivity, and nontemporal quiescence of the resultant photographic image, and because of the deeply-rooted satisfaction to be gained from creating images generally assumed not merely to reflect or represent but actually to be the truth.

By example of his own apparent confidence and the casual ease with which he seemed to approach life, he taught her to be less fearful; and because of the breadth and intensity of her fears, he praised her excessively for overcoming them in small ways, ironically celebrating her stalwartness and bravery, while in truth those things were by considerable measure the lesser, not the greater, part of her character.

It seemed to him, and he made a note of it in writing, apparently without embarrassment or self-consciousness, that life between them was a slow, unrushed study of how to live life, she the observant student, he the experimenter and master.

Their dog: a small, deep-copper-colored dachshund that he named Shilling rather than Penny, as being more exotic. The photograph of him on the top step of the front porch with the small dog curled in his lap. He has taken up the smoking of briar pipes, and he holds one now firmly in his teeth as he gazes at the camera. He leans back, his hands on the porch floor behind him. Once again, there is the expression of light, controlled, slightly ironic amusement on his face, but with a faint suggestion of emptiness in its handsome, too consciously posed contentedness: movie star, actor, with panic somewhere underneath, the other face looking out.

Children would not begin to arrive for six years. This reluctance was his, defended with a thin logic and facile dialectic that appeared in no other area of his life: the world was not ready for children, perhaps it never would be, how to justify bringing new life into a world of hypocrisy, danger, ugliness, instability. His real reasons, however, must have been other than these, more private, since it was clear to anyone who knew him well that he was not political. Spain and Germany were images of wineskins and dry sunlight, half-timbered inns, forested mountains. He thought through mood, not idea: summer sunlight, evening breeze over dry earth, scent of coming rain. He read Ernest Hemingway, Eugene O'Neill, Edna St. Vincent Millay, Willa Cather, Sherwood Anderson, Robinson Jeffers. In recurrent periods of inexplicable intensity, he devoted himself to the writing of lyric, derivative short stories that he mailed to regional magazines of the

Depression years that were trying to sustain a quixotic belief in the virility and drive of a native, land-rooted, class-free populist art.

June 18th, 1933; August 9th, 1934; January 21st, 1936; July 7th, 1937; August 24th, 1938. Time not passing, time passing.

The photographs from these years, almost without exception, suggest a world of calmness, pastoral quietness, hushed motionlessness, and a subtly controlled, not as yet wholly rigidified, but a carefully protected impersonality. The photographs are by no means without pleasure, interest, or even occasional charm, yet in them one senses always the subtle presence of a distractingly excessive control of a peculiarly emotional and yet at the same time chilling kind, an almost too great and perhaps a compulsive seeking for an already imagined perfection in each image and in the composition of each frame, with the result

He embarked upon an ambitious series of photographs of the surface, from various angles, of his own desk—the chair in each case pushed back in just such a way as to suggest the mysterious absence of its unseen proprietor. Manuscript pages placed in changing positions; a briar pipe placed here, then there; a cigarette on the lip of an ashtray, its smoke rising smoothly through a shaft of sunlight, the half-empty packet lying nearby; an open book, reading glasses on its surface; an empty wine glass; a fountain pen left lying across a typed sheet, showing strike-outs and corrections under the soft light of a shaded desk lamp. Most of the photographs are from close up; in others, the camera has drawn back to reveal an open window nearby, across the room. He entitled the series "Studies in Light."

She was intelligent, poised, and attractive, but underlying these traits were the timidity and passiveness that had themselves drawn him to her with equal strength. She was easily contented. Although far from ignorant, she had never believed herself in any way ambitious, and for this reason she was undemanding. For her, life consisted of those things that happened to her; passive, accepting, and easily contented, it did not occur to her that she might live in another way, that by the unceasing exertion of her will she might herself determine the nature of those things that would happen to her. Thus for him she was a figure of seeming perfection; contented and satisfied herself with her unexamined belief in his future greatness, she would never demand of him that he take action. He could speak openly of his endless and varied desires—to live in Europe, to travel by sea, to seek adventure, to experience the exotic life—with the keen pleasure of having always an enraptured listener, yet with the equal confidence that she would never herself take fire and press him unremittingly to act. For him, here were both satisfaction and safety; here he could lead dramatically without showing the way; here was a subtle perfection—if only because within it nothing would ever happen—of freedom.

A street at night during snowfall, deserted, at the far end a street lamp shedding its light; rain on abandoned windowglass, one pane broken; the milkman's wagon, his dappled horse with blinders; patterns of breaking ice on the smooth black surface of the river; the old-fashioned, three-faced clock suspended over the wooden doorway to the bank; sunlight on weathered clapboards; a deserted farmhouse; the silence of tall grass on a prairie hillside in high summer (only in much later years would he grow to despise her for the very timidity he had earlier treasured and which, for his own needs, he had flattered—deriding her with an undisguised cruelty of tone for those small things she would never be able to do: drive an automobile, stand at the overlook of a cliff, see a carving knife sharpened without wincing, ride without whitened knuckles in a boat, travel far from home without dread).

that there is in them always the faintest suggestion of the artificial, not in a crude or obvious sense, but to the extent that one never loses a faint awareness of self-consciousness in viewing these images, discovering in them the sense of an artist too little spontaneous and too little generous in responding to the full breadth, flavor, and texture, and especially to the range, of human losses, failures, and imperfections of his era, without which any corpus of art, however skilled in its execution, will in the end be felt to be miniaturized, limited, held back, too little trusting and human, trivialized, too little alive.

He took up new interests with a quality of ceremony, a seriousness, and a detailed formality that made each of them for a time all-consuming and that imbued them with a mysterious aura of weighty significance that he never explained and that she never questioned. He became a committed golfer, dressed in plus-fours and white shoes, practiced putting on the carpet, studied his swings, spent long afternoons on the course. He played tennis, cross-country skied on rigorous full-day journeys. He became a sport fisherman, bought hip waders, a soft hat, flannel shirts, a trout basket and net, spent long nighttime hours at a table in the kitchen hand-tying flies. He became a hunter and gathered about him a shot-gun, boots, bush pants, a jacket with shell loops on the breast and with loose pockets in the lining to carry felled birds. He expanded his library, had *ex libris* nameplates printed, and pasted one carefully inside the cover of each of his books. He began a journal of his daily life, then abandoned it. He took up jazz piano, practicing intently through the long hours of the night into dawn.

The element of costume: trying on, discarding, withdraw-ing, seeking always a new wardrobe. Standing for a time in the lights to draw attention, suggest focus and direction, be bold, yet arranging things carefully underneath so that nothing will ever quite happen, the play will never be con-cluded: the actor, pointing elsewhere, will slip out the back way, silently pleased with himself at his quick deflection of the audience's attention, his own swiftness of foot, his escape, the success again of his failure to define himself.

A long drama of beginnings: an extended season of sum-mer, a filling of radiant youth with a void of charmed time.

And yet of course his true aim never was to embrace or to be inclusive. He did not seek a truly generative art, but rather he sought to narrow, proscribe, pin down, to capture the desirable elements of the mute, poised, and unmolested world of which he perceived himself to be the center. Above all, his aim was to arrest time; it was the romantic's coldly fevered desire to seize life at a given hour, embrace the poised resonance of that single immutable moment, and sacrifice all else. In this need, the camera suited him well, being an instrument that in itself would not struggle against the restrictiveness, narrowness, or doomed paradox of his aim.

Automobile. 1937. Maroon Ford coupé. The automobile is an imaginative treasure to him, and he fantasizes with her now (late at night, at the kitchen table by an open window, over a plate of cold fried chicken, beaded glasses of ale to drink) of New York City, San Francisco, New Orleans, Montreal, the mountains of Denver, the Pacific Northwest, the Catskills of his boyhood vacations, the Blue Mountains, the Spanish Southwest, Mexico, the coast of Maine, Nova Scotia (he stops the car in isolated places: on the tops of hills with undulating prairie vistas; overlooking the tree-lined valleys of meandering streams; on quiet roadsides near abandoned and weathered country churches).

She is not perturbed or troubled by his speaking so frequently of travel, of plans, vague and insistent desires to be other and to be elsewhere that lead inevitably to nothing. She listens. She does not question. She does not scrutinize deeply any element of his behavior or character, and she finds therefore in these contented years of luxury and sunlit ease no hint of the quietly coiled morbidity that lies within them—no more than she sees symbols of small deaths in the abandoned costumes that accumulate behind him like empty husks: his fishing gear tangled on cellar rafters, skis left warping in a corner by the furnace, hunting clothes mildewing in a wooden crate, golf clubs lying under dust on the attic floor, his shotgun uncased and slowly rusting at the back of the front hall closet.

She rides with him for circuitous tens of miles, entire summer days, in the countryside around West Tree, Minnesota. The stops he makes are sometimes long. Contented, patient, languorous in the warmth of the sunlight, she waits. She suns her legs in the open car door, raises her chin to expose her throat. The engine of the car ticks quietly as it cools. Nearby, a meadowlark perches on a weathered fencepost, surveys for danger, raises its beak, and with its bibbed throat pulsing, warbles its falling song. Again. And again. Then the meadowlark flies. In the hushed, newly intensified quietness of the warm afternoon, she watches the photographer in the distance, standing in a field of knee-high grass, hunched slightly forward over his wooden tripod, his head and shoulders (as if held below the waters of a small dark sea) invisible under the folds of heavy black cloth.

It must be admitted that with the aid of the camera, whatever his real aims may have been, he did create a certain balanced and ironically austere preciosity, a peculiarly indulgent and yet impersonal, secretive and yet thinly romantic delicacy of aesthetic nostalgia. There is in it, of course, the governing and dominant irony of the moribund. For even now, forty or more years after their creation, we look at these innumerable pastoral photographs of the Middle West of the 1930s, and inevitably, in spite of our better judgment and without hope of success, we find ourselves attempting to imagine, recapture, seize again the exact moment in abandoned, echoless, irretrievably lost time when the eye of the doomed photographer saw precisely what we now see. For to do so is, of course, to look once again through the very eye of the man now dead: to see autumn leaves scattered on wet paving stones in rain; a sharply drawn shadow of tree trunk curving austerely over unbroken sunlit snow; new wildflowers rising out of dead matted grass in spring; a farmer pitching a bundle of ripe wheat up onto his horse-drawn wagon, the raised tines of his fork poised in sunlight, the bundle of grain suspended for eternity in air under the high cloudless dome of calm, perfected summer sky.

NOTEBOOK

We were born, Hannah and Ingie and I,
one of us after another, and that changed
everything. Our voices, our questions,
made time move; bit by bit, we forced the
past to withdraw. There was a certain
horror in this. Best would have been to
keep us quiet, set us back on the shelf,
close the door. How sad it was, after all,
this terrible pretending about life, pre-
tending that it doesn't change.

   And we had our stories, of course, the
three of us.

FIVE
(1942–1946)

Ingie

There was great excitement; we mimicked it. After the news came over the radio, I marched with my brother and sister along the curb in front of the house, banging the lids of saucepans together like cymbals. In the living room my mother wept, her face cradled in her hands; the woman next door, standing at her porch rail, banged the bottom of an empty spaghetti pot with a wooden spoon. Across the street three boys lit firecrackers. They squatted down on the lawn, then leapt into the gathering dusk away from the brief point of white light and the bang. Downtown, two blocks away, there was the sound of honking horns, and, for a time, the unsteady pealing of a bell.

Men came back one by one from the edges of the earth; there were reunions in one house and then another. When my father came home, he put his visored cap with its heavy metal eagle on each of our heads, one after the other, and our pictures were taken. He opened his crumpled leather bag, showed us paper rolls of Japanese money, a spent artillery cartridge of brass, three miniature black elephants with their tusks tipped in smooth white ivory. At dinner the first night, pleasantly satisfied with eating, he leaned back in his chair, sighed deeply, and loosened his belt. After some time, my mother became pregnant.

.

The middle child, I had spent the years of his absence dressing up in clothing from my mother's bureau and from her bedroom closet: the silken material of blouses cascaded over my thin bare arms; strings of heavy beads descended from my neck; the great lengths of her dresses and her yellow bathrobe trailed behind me over the polished wooden floor as I posed before the mirror hung on the door of the closet. (Gray daylight came through the panes of tall windows in the room. Small photographs were stuck around the edges of the mirror on my mother's dresser.)

.

Time passed slowly. On weekdays I walked home from school in the stillness and silence of noon for bowls of warm soup. Going past empty lawns in front of large quiet houses, I observed closed garage doors, tightly curtained windows, high pointed gables reaching toward a gray sky. In the evenings after dinner my mother read aloud to us or sat on the sofa knitting sweaters and mittens while I played imaginary games on the living room carpet with my brother and sister, and the furnace droned and hummed in the basement, warming the house against the cold outdoors.

.

In subtle, unspoken ways his unhappiness with the future in store for him colored the atmosphere of our lives. In late autumn, when it grew dark early and the air outdoors was chill, he would sit with my mother at the kitchen table and talk about the choices he would like to make. They drank glasses of whiskey while food steamed in saucepans on the stove. During these conversations their voices sometimes dropped low, and my mother turned her glass around slowly on the table in front of her, looking down into it.

Once, when I entered the kitchen to find them sitting entirely in silence, neither of them looking at the other, my father put out his arm in sudden joviality, pulled me up close against his side, and said,

"Well, Ingie, how would you like to move to a big white house by the ocean, high up on a green hill, and have your daddy be in the navy again and sail on ships and send you presents from all over the world?"

Awkward and somewhat embarrassed by the unexpected suddenness of his rough embrace, I watched as my mother, in one motion, pushed back her chair and stood up with the quickness of anger and impatience to busy herself at the stove. She kept her back toward us and said nothing; but in spite of her injured silence it was years before I understood the depth of my father's regret at the war's having come to an end, and his continued longing for something eventful and dramatic to enter again into his life.

.

At first his return was like having a guest in the house. He was unfamiliar to us, fresh and exotic. We stood in a cluster at the bathroom door upstairs to watch him while he shaved, then followed him into the bedroom to see him dress. He was amused by us, laughed warmly, treated us to small indulgences. We wore his shoes, felt the roughness of his face, accepted touches of scented shaving lotion behind our ears. He allowed us to examine his cuff links, wear his jackets, even to study the contents of his pants pockets—the Zippo lighter, the pile of loose change, the slender penknife with its single blade, his key chain in the shape of a tiny ship with the keys suspended from its anchor. This mood, however, changed gradually, almost without our noticing it. As time went on, he touched our heads less frequently, he raised us in his arms only seldom, we heard his laughter less often. As the weeks went by, and then the months, the bedroom door came to be closed, and my father no longer joined us at the table for breakfast.

•

Nothing was going to happen. After great sound, upheaval, the rise and clashing of nations, unspeakable terror, the world seemed suddenly not to breathe, to be still. It was as if the nature of drama itself had changed. My father, burdened with loss and regret, tried in vain to imagine what the remainder of his life would bring. In his thoughts, he traveled to the far edges of the earth, traversing the wide oceans in pursuit of clarity and romance, leaving us behind in the stillness of the small town, sheltered safely in our wood-frame house.

•

They did not quarrel. There was not the drama of raised voices in the night. My father did not abandon my mother. There was not violence between them. Very little happened, not enough for a story.

In March, my mother became ill with her pregnancy; a woman came to the house to attend her in the daytime, while, in obedience to the doctor's orders, she remained in bed.

•

Shortly after Christmas my father returned to his job at my grandfather's movie theater; he was away from the house in the evenings and slept late in the mornings. Time passed slowly and very little seemed to have changed. On weekdays I walked home from school in the stillness and silence of noon for bowls of warm soup. Passing empty lawns in front of large quiet houses, I observed closed front doors, primly curtained windows, high pointed gables reaching toward a cold sky. In the evenings after dinner my mother read aloud to us or lay against pillows on the sofa knitting sweaters and mittens while on the living room carpet my brother and sister and I played games devised of imaginary characters, and in the basement below us the furnace droned and hummed quietly, warming the house against the silent cold outdoors.

·

(Lying one night on the sofa, as the doctor required, my mother thought she smelled smoke in the air, a subtle flavor of density and heat that she couldn't be certain of. At last she raised herself from the sofa and climbed the stairs, holding the hem of her long yellow bathrobe gathered in one hand. Near the top, she gave a sharp exclamation in sudden fear, and, turning quickly to come down, stepped on the hem of the robe and fell. She reached out for the railing but missed it; her body rolling and turning, she fell terribly to the landing at the bottom of the stairs, where she lay crumpled on the floor, the yellow gown, having briefly filled with air, collapsed and soft around her. For a moment there was the awful silence of nothingness. Then she started to move, not rising from the floor, where she lay on her side, but seeming almost invisibly to draw herself more tightly together. Her eyes were closed.

"Run for your father," she whispered to Hannah and me.

Outdoors, the night air was icy, and patches of thawed snow gleamed pale in the darkness. We ran holding hands,

Hannah pulling me behind her. She was dressed still in her school clothes, but I wore only a pair of slippers and my blue cotton nightgown, which billowed out behind me in the icy air as we ran.

From the top of the Fourth Street hill a block away, we could see the theater, with its glass doors, square marquee, and its rows of small lightbulbs that by blinking seemed to ripple in movement. We turned down the hill. My father stood in the recessed doorway of the old stage entrance on Fourth Street, leaning there, as he habitually did, smoking a cigarette and looking out into the night while the movie played itself through, tinkling and frothy, on the other side of the closed door behind him. Standing there alone, dressed in his herringbone suit and gleaming shoes, poised suavely with one shoulder against the side of the doorway as he gazed off into the night, perhaps he was dreaming of Manila, the white beaches of Tahiti, the soft night air of the Hawaiian Islands as we ran down the hill to find him. Hannah shouted out as we ran. My father dropped his cigarette, then pressed it under his toe as he turned out of the doorway and took a step or two toward us. For a brief moment, as we drew nearer, there was an expression of pleased amusement on his face, but then quickly that changed, and we were up to him and tugging at his hands and telling him: *Mother fell down the stairs and the house has caught on fire.*

.

When we got back, the fire truck was parked at the curb, its red light pulsing lazily on top of the cab. Black smoke that breathed out bright red sparks and flickering lily pads of soft flame rose from the chimney on the high peak of the house and drifted hurriedly up into the night sky. Firemen went in and out of the basement through an open cellar door. Others had placed a high ladder against a wall and were climbing it to the roof.

In the living room, my mother had been placed on a stretcher; two men tightened webbed belts over her ankles, and another stood by, holding Malcolm by the hand, both of them watching. She was carried out, my father holding the door open awkwardly, trying to squeeze himself out of the way of the firemen and the passing stretcher. My mother's eyes were shut tightly, as though she heard nothing around her and was aware of no one, but was concentrating on something inward, something more important than anything else, a problem that was unspeakably difficult.

·

From the front window, I watched the white ambulance they put her in move away. My father ran around the corner of the house to the garage, backed out the car, and followed. With my forehead pressed against the cold, smooth glass of the front window, I looked out into the alarm of the night. I knew there were men on the roof of the house, and others in the basement. The red taillights of my father's small Ford, moving down the darkened street as though pulled swiftly along by an invisible string, grew smaller, diminished, then disappeared. This was in 1946. I was six years old. I remember my mother's white knuckles as she gripped the rails of the stretcher, the unfamiliar look of alarm and fear on my father's face as he held open the door, and the people from the neighborhood, after the ambulance was gone, moving up closer from the edges of the night to gaze in at us where we stood, as if captured, inside the lighted windows of our house.)

SIX

(1947–1951)

Malcolm

I

Consider the vulnerability of the farm: unlike a roof, the sky offers it no protection from above; unshielded by hills, it is subject to the ravages of prairie wind, of blizzard, dust, and arctic cold; its crops are vulnerable to squall, hail, drought, flood, depletion of the soil, plague of insect or blight; its livestock are prone to madness, deformation, accident, and disease; its finances are most frequently overextended, its profits tenuous or nonexistent. The farm, it seems, gazes always into the open mouth of doom, can be destroyed with relative ease by forces that come from within or from without. As a symbol, it is considered traditionally to be ancient, suggestive, and rich in multitudinous meanings.

Not long after the end of World War II, in the autumn of the year 1947, my father moved with his family to a small farm two and a half miles north of West Tree.

II

September 20th, 1947. My father draws the car slowly to a stop on the shoulder of the gravel road. He leans forward to set the handbrake, then turns off the engine. Through the rolled-down windows of the car, we gaze at the farmhouse where it stands silently behind the deep, flat apron of its front lawn.

It is made of white clapboard, and it is in need of paint. Two upstairs gables face the road, and the tall sash windows set into them gaze back at us without recognition. The windows are curtainless. Behind them is the flat, empty darkness of an uninhabited house.

Atop the house is a brick chimney. On the front is a low porch with square wooden posts supporting its slanted roof. From the limb of a tree on the front lawn hangs a swing made of a single rope and a rubber tire. Under the swing, the grass of the lawn is worn into a shallow oval basin of bare dirt.

In the front seat of the car, my father lights a cigarette. I catch the scent of the freshly lighted tobacco. My father exhales. The smoke hits the windshield, then spreads out against the glass.

From the lowering sun in the west, long shadows of tree trunks fall in silent bands across the tracks of the driveway as they disappear around to the back of the empty farmhouse.

·

(In winter, the old house labored frequently under the ponderous blows of a north wind. At night, when I could feel the wall beside my bed shuddering under its force, I would listen in fear to the screaming and cavernous sounds of the rising storm. In the morning, looking out from the window of my upstairs room, I would see thickly veiled air churning and swept with bright whiteness. Deep drifts of snow, whirled and dropped by the wind, would be slowly filling up the sheltered center of the farmyard. Smooth inclines of snow mounted the sides of the unpainted wooden sheds, obscured all but the tops of their doorways, covered their windows, sometimes reached to their sagging rooftops.

Sometimes we were snowbound for days at a time. After the passing of the storm, the air calmed slowly and the temperature dropped below zero. Under a black sky flung across with bright stars, the nights were frozen into an immaculate emptiness of poised, hushed silence. The farmhouse shrank in the still, arctic cold, settling into itself after the fierceness of the wind like an old tooth settling back into its socket. Lying awake in the vast silence, I would sometimes hear the sharp rifle-crack of a freezing tree limb, a single echoless report from somewhere outside in the blue and shadowed darkness.)

III

The farm was a graveyard of symbols. When we moved into the house, there was discovered in the low attic over the kitchen the white, thin-boned skeleton of a squirrel, at that time the house's only tenant. Outdoors, ancient fences were in need of repair; rotted free at their bases, fence posts leaned against the restraint of barbed wire and attempted to lie down on the ground in rows like toppled grave markers. Near a corner of the house stood an elm tree whose flesh had grown around the shaft of a thick iron bolt, absorbing it more and more deeply year after year until at last it disappeared into the puckered wound and was lost from sight.

Symbols of rural antiquity, of time having come to a stop on the old farm. In soft moss alongside the shaft of a rotted tree trunk grew violets, larkspur, bloodroot, and ferns. A

grove of trees stood to the west of the farmhouse as a wind-
break; there, in tall grass, lay the bleached white skull of a
cow, empty-eyed and with curved horns, sunlight touching it
through the movement of leaves overhead. This farm, it was
clear, had once held life. Near the driveway, hooked from
the low branch of a pine, hung a large scythe, as if once,
years before, a farmer had ended his day's work at that precise place and hung his implement there: its long, curved
blade was roughened now with dark rust, its sinuous bent-
wood handle weathered, cracked, and bleached.

My father craved these emblems of arrested antiquity and
endeavored to keep them, insofar as possible, unaltered and
untouched. In this desire he was rigid, possessive, and unforgiving. The farm represented a perfected world within
which he attempted to enclose himself, and he became enraged at my sisters or me if, in the carelessness of our play,
we touched or altered these symbols that surrounded him: if
we moved the bleached skull, trampled with our feet the frail
and rotted hollowness of the old tree trunk, or, in the irrev-
erent and careless pleasures of our childhood, set the rusty
scythe swinging merrily on its branch.

IV

(*You were not close to your father during these years?*)
My father was a symbol, his origins shrouded in obscurity
and mystery, his dominance absolute and not to be questioned. Most notable about him in these years was his displeasure: swift to arise, unqualified in its intensity. It seems
to me now that life on the farm had as its deepest regulat-
ing principle the avoiding of that displeasure; the moments

of gaiety or lightness that occurred were the moments of un-expected and temporary release from its threat.

·

I was six years old when my family moved to the farm. My father taught me to identify the types of clouds in the open prairie sky above us: cirrus, stratus, cumulus, nimbus. He observed with me the prairie winds, their direction and force; he gave me a copy of the Beaufort Scale with its con-cise descriptions of the winds and their observable effects from light air through fresh breeze to gale, storm, and hur-ricane. He allowed me to ride beside him on the fender of our gray Ford tractor as he drove into the fields, or to ride behind him in the hitched wagon. In the farmyard I did chores, sharing the work with my father. I carried pails of water for the penned calves. I swept the floor of the barn, afterwards sprinkling cool handfuls of fresh white lime on the damp cement floor. On summer afternoons my father took me with him on long, meandering journeys in the car, when he drove slowly through the countryside, on narrow back roads, in search of photographs. He stopped at abandoned country churches, neglected cemeteries on grass-covered hills, empty farmhouses, where he set up his tripod and disappeared for long times under the heavy black cloth that he placed over his head, while I waited for him, afraid to speak of my boredom or to allow it to show.

·

I desired: my father's approval, intimacy, and kindness. I feared: his wrath, sullenness, crippling scorn. In order to avoid these things, I became adept at effacing myself. At those times when I was most fearful, I spoke little, walked softly, pursued a detailed and fastidious obedience, stifled complaints, made few requests. These practices, however, were not invariably successful, and with some frequency during these years on the farm I sought out places in which to hide. Among these were the low attic over the kitchen, the quiet hayloft of the barn, and certain copses and dirt-floored thickets in the wooded areas that, on various sides, surrounded the old farmhouse.)

V

I stand in the barn watching while my father pitches loose hay through the trapdoor from the hayloft above. When the first forkfuls land on the bare cement floor, dust rises up, and the cattle raise their heads to gaze toward the deepening pile of their food. On rare occasions, when a bundle of hay first strikes the floor, small mice scatter outward, shaken from their nests. These are leapt upon in their flight by wary and observant cats, who consume their prey comfortably in the corners of the barn, small bones cracking quietly between sharp teeth.

My father's rage could leap forth similarly, often without warning or visible cause. In the barn, he was tolerant of the animals, kindly toward the cowering black dog, the large sleepy cows chewing their cuds in their metal stanchions, until something in their stupidity, their unresponsiveness, their animal slowness—something in their *existing*—tripped him into vast rage. I watched him lash them furiously across their snouts, kick at their hamstrings, whip their broad backs with leather straps, curses flying from his mouth.

He once swung his foot to kick a full bucket, the noise and movement causing the cattle, in sudden alarm, to lurch and pull noisily in their stanchions. My father's blow sent a thick, ductile arc of milk high into the air and the bucket itself into a corner of the barn, where he pursued it further, his rage not spent, while cats slunk out cautiously behind him to lap the spilled milk.

VI

My father was not political, even though in his thinking he was wide-reaching, and even though he generalized bitterly and habitually about the world, narrating its story in categories of broad, monolithic, almost entirely negative forces: worldwide greed for profit, universal ignorance and benightedness, arrant grasping for power both in nations and in their leaders. No political figure, however grand or obscure, was free in my father's view from the suspicion of arrogance and greed, or from the charge, inevitably, of seeking power not for the sake of doing good but for the sake of holding power alone.

Yet in his Manichaean view of history's downward spiral, my father was remarkably unspecific. The world existed; its vast forces pressed painfully upon my father's angry but morally sensitive spirit; and still he seemed to have little interest in the details of those forces, in the politics of his age. Politics for my father, whatever great breadth of books he had read or would continue to read during his life, was a matter not for study or analysis, but a feeling, a gloom, a generalized belief in a single vast force quite entirely beyond the control of any opposing and humane principle. My father, in his passion, tended not to make distinctions. The European holocaust, the destruction of Hitler, the division of Germany, the creation of Israel, the socialist program in England, the Chinese revolution, the independence of India, the evolving policy of the Soviet Union under late Stalinism, the development of the hydrogen bomb: vaguely differentiated events in the hopeless, doomed, slowly spiraling cosmos.

·

(In the early hours of a blizzard, the light outdoors became airy and bright, flooding through the windows to fill the house with a clear and Alpine whiteness. I spent one of these white-lighted afternoons in my room building a wooden model of the battleship *New Jersey*. After supper, when night had fallen, I climbed the stairs once again to cut miniature gun turrets from chips of balsa wood and to make cannon barrels and rigging from the tips of straight pins and small bits of thread. As I worked, the pitch of the storm outdoors heightened, then rose to such an intensity that I grew afraid. The wind whistled in rising tones. It pounded with a malevolent brutishness at the house, caused the walls to shudder, rattled windows, raced screaming up the slope of the roof. I left my desk, afraid any longer to stay alone, and went downstairs. My father lay on the sofa in a darkened room, a single lamp shedding light on the book he was reading. I spoke and approached him, but he showed no recognition that I was there. I went nearer, but, absorbed in his reading, he remained as if still unaware of my presence. I went to the edge of the sofa and sat down on the floor, looking up at his face. Still he took no notice of me. It was as though I were not there. While the wind screamed outdoors, battering at the farmhouse in sweeping fury, I watched in silence the tiny, flickering movements of my father's eyes as they moved with silent, spider-like hunger and quickness from word to word, from line to line, of his book.

A decade later, when I went to college and stayed up late one night reading Thoreau, who had lived a hundred years before at Walden Pond, in the solitude of his small cabin, reading his books, I thought of this: I thought of the silent, eager, flickering movement of my father's eyes.)

VII

How much anger there was in my father: something in him made him wish to destroy himself, to destroy others as well, to pull down the world around him and trample it in angry spite. Throughout his life he wrestled with this desire, sought to contain the terrible impulse of rage, yet at the same time fed on it secretly as if from a silent pool of irresistable liquor that lay hidden deeply inside himself. My father's life was a short circuit, a trip-valve, a contradiction: he must be in rage, yet he must not be in rage; he must rise in the world, he must not rise in the world; he must exist, yet he must not exist. My father *agonistes*: his emotional life a ganglionlike bondage of knots that grew tighter and more unrelieving with the struggle. There were times—in winter, on the farm, in the bottom of despair—when I imagine, had my father been an animal, that he would have devoured us one at a time, then slunk into his lair to gnaw slowly with sullen and furious spite at his own limbs and flesh.

.

I think this now, many years later, of my father: He had cast off boldly the husk and fraudulent pomp of his father's and his forefathers' religion; but the ineradicable and inborn sinews of its guilt still remained, as did the dark shadow behind the center of his heart—hidden out of the reach of words and, silently, beyond the realm of thought itself—

reminding him unceasingly that he was a soul doomed and insolent and condemned. Only in half measure was my father the child of his stern fathers. And only in half measure was he their rebellious son. Confusion, a shambles of misidentities lay beneath his sternness and his outward show of control. Below the surface of my unrelenting father were contradiction, madness, loss, and the unappeasable and impossible rage of the orphan and the unforgiven.

VIII

Love: In his moments of rage, my father did not strike us. In the chronicle of these pastoral years, there is no homely or pathetic saga of physical tyranny, of beatings in drunken anger, of weeping children, of bruised and pale wives. My father's rage caused him to burst the kitchen door from its hinges; it caused him to crack the dining room table in half with furious swings of his foot; to kick Ganges, the strangely-named and cowering black dog, in the ribs as it fawned on its belly toward him in the barnyard, eyes upturned, tail sweeping the dust. But our own bodies, evidence of the love he bore us in his torment, escaped these blows.

He did not, in times even of happiness or levity, touch us. The pat on the head, the squeeze of the arm, touching of the hand, the embrace, lifting up, tossing in the air, these were unknown in the experience of growing up with my father.

His consistency of physical restraint and withdrawal seems to me now astonishing, unnatural, extreme. And yet perhaps it was this: perhaps he did not touch his children because he could not tolerate, did not know how to bear, the knowledge that such touching gave him: the pathetic, rending, devastating self-knowledge that these children had been brought into

existence, that they were his, that he had caused them, that
they were there.

IX

Alcohol: Rage existed in my father; it did not require the
fanning of liquor to breathe it into life. A great deal of drink,
in fact, had a dramatically opposite effect on my father. Alcohol slowed something down inside him, dropped guards,
opened switches, allowed thick floods of emotion and warmth
to come through.

My father labored under great extremes in all things, and
in his drunkenness he labored under the awesome intensity
of his interconnectedness with all existence, his oneness with
the cosmos. This awareness in my father was expressed in
drunkenness with the emotional excess and the immodest un-
guardedness of relief after great pain. On hot summer nights
at the round oak table in the dining room, windows raised
to the night air, the many doors of the old farmhouse standing opened wide to the darkness outside, music playing on
the phonograph from my father's collection of jazz from the
1930s, the family gathers for a party. There are gin and ton-
ics, the rare treat of Coca-Colas for the children, plates of
cheese and crackers and tins of sardines on the table. Early,
before he begins, after still more drink, to devote himself
solely to the music, my father presents himself to us in a way
that we very seldom see. We listen quietly as he delivers
to us, in the excessive honesty of the drinker, intense and
weaving dissertations on his depths of love, guilt, remorse,
fear, awe, regret, sorrow. As he drinks more, his awareness of an audience diminishes, disappears, and yet he keeps
talking, repeating, apologizing, confessing. Sometimes, just

before the music captures him entirely, there are tears and brief weeping, more frequently only a moistness in the plaint of the dark eyes that are turned shallow from the liquor.

.

We see him at these times as passive, selfless, humble, groping, his hands spread flat on the table's surface, caressing its grain as if he is seeking some tangible way to express the feelings bursting in his heart. Rage has disappeared, it seems just now never to have existed, it occurs to no one now to remember it. The evening grows longer. The gin disappears, a half bottle of whiskey is gotten from a cupboard. There is a subtle change in the atmosphere of the night; my father puts a new stack of records on the phonograph, and he is captured by the music, swept up by it, expanded by it out to the farthest edges of the universe from where he sits in the bare and underfurnished dining room in the farmhouse in Minnesota. The rest of us are forgotten, and my father no longer uses words, only gestures and sounds. If he had used words, he would have said, as if in a sermon or a prayer: Let us now immerse ourselves in the infinite pathos of life, its beauty, grandeur, inspiration, its awesomeness. Let us rise, let us be swept upward! A high, smooth wave is curling over us, higher, higher, sorrow, beauty, greatness, ambition, and we are lifted up; we flounder at first, and then we swim with great simplicity and ease in the green-blue and light-filled upsweeping sea, its warmth, its grace, its enormous height. Bechet! Dodds! The immortal and golden-toned Beiderbeck, dead in youth! Teagarden! Hampton! Goodman! The world! The past! All of life! All of death! Come with me! Join with me!

.

On these summer nights, I would sometimes watch my father closely. Sitting on a chair in the middle of the bare room, he would follow the music in a kind of intense and prolonged ecstasy, its phrasings, the interweaving of its sounds, the complex and passionately controlled intensity as it built and rose to climax after climax. My father would not rise from his chair; but he would clench his fists, extend his arms, arch his back, and slowly, painfully, writhe his body and his extended limbs as the music swept into him, his eyes squeezed tightly shut, his sweating face raised to heaven, his mouth wrenched in a smiling grimace of tight, sweet, bursting agony.

X

On mornings after drinking, my father is sullen. He is clamped terribly in a grim, tinderlike rage of virulence and scorn at the exposure of the evening before, the failure to keep control, the exhibition of unguarded feeling. Sometimes entire days will pass—two days, three—when he does not speak a word, not even at meals, not even at bedtime. The world shrinks at these times into a chill crevice of fear. During these times, we move about the house with the cautiousness, wariness, and quietness of mice, keeping out of his sight insofar as we are able, terrified of him, of his wrath, of his wish that we had not seen him, his wish that we did not exist.

.

He avoided looking at us or meeting our eyes at these times, or if he did look, it was with a withering and scornful gaze, suggestive of inexpressible disgust. My father's, toward us, was a brutality almost entirely intellectual, the fruit of his heritage, without fists, without cruel hands, without curses, without swinging boots. Yet a mere look from him at these times carried what seemed indisputably an equally heavy burden of meaning, a burden made only heavier by the constraint of unbroken wordlessness that surrounded it, in which the sounds of our silverware and dishes seemed to bang and reverberate clumsily, hopelessly drawing attention to us— the glance of sullen, sickened displeasure as he looks up at me from his plate, the unforgiving scorn in the coldness of the steady eyes, then without a word the lowered gaze, as if not a moment more of such a sight could be borne: *that boy, repugnant, eating peas from his plate, hunched uncouthly over his meal, making small sounds in the silence with his mouth as he eats, that boy offends me, I wish he were dead.*

(Sometimes in late afternoon he would lie on the sofa with a book, and then, while reading, fall asleep. My father was not a man who took his leisure freely. I believe that I never saw him sleeping in this way—on the sofa, in the daytime— except with an open book, the sign of work remaining undone, resting face down on the rise and fall of his chest.

At these times my mother would say to us with a quiet and urgent protectiveness in her voice, if we should come into the room or enter the house from outdoors: *Be careful. Hush. Be quiet. Don't wake your father.*)

XI

Let him sleep, let him find respite, let him rest for a time. It was to require a decade for the farm to fail entirely: by that time only the house would be lived in by my family; the farmland would be rented to others; the barn and outbuildings would be empty, wind-haunted, beginning their long slow fall into weathered ruin and collapse. My father by then would be almost fifty years old. He would at last return to his books, and, choosing that particular way to seize once again at timelessness with his hands, become a teacher at the college in West Tree.

The farm was a necessity for my father, a requirement for that decade of his life. When he moved there in 1947, I believe that, in some terrible recognition of what waited for him in the future, he wished to step outside of time altogether. The farm was a doomed attempt to grasp at an idea that existed with vague brilliance somewhere in my father's mythic past, an attempt to hold that idea motionless, keep it still, prevent it from getting away: a distantly remembered idyll, a clearly focused image of sun-warmed radiance from an elusive corner of his childhood, a place in time where for a charmed moment there had been no struggle, no conflict, no loss.

Even in the coldest, locked-in depths of the winter, the air in the barn stayed moist and warm from the cattle's breathing and from the heat of their huge, slow bodies. I lingered there until well after the early sunset while my father finished the chores, milked the cows, pitched hay and silage into their troughs. On the inside of the barn door that was shut against the cold, the heads of iron bolts sprouted thick white growths of frost, like the white fur hats of royal guards. On the windowpanes over the calves' pens the soft frost grew to the depth of my first knuckle.

In the farmhouse, it seemed even colder, and we struggled to keep warm. Cold air seeped upward from the bare linoleum of the floors, and it found its way in around loose window frames, bringing with it the chill fresh scent of ice. In the kitchen, butter set out on the table failed to soften. It was too cold in the kitchen for bread to rise, and glass jars of preserves set on shelves against the outside wall of the pantry froze and cracked.

My sister Hannah sat reading on a stool in the dining room, where warm air rose up through a forced-air register from the laboring furnace in the cellar. Her long black hair, electrified by the dry air, stood out from her head and clung in a wide spray to the pale flowered wallpaper behind her, making her seem like a quietly posing figure of young madness or fear. My father took photographs of her there as she smiled for him, cocked an eyebrow, looked up coyly over the edge of her book.

There were times when the house seemed our common fortress against a frozen wilderness that reached outward to the low circle of the horizons. We waited patiently for the slow change in season, spoke quietly, laughed contentedly as we ate our meals together in the kitchen warmed by the heated oven. We went to bed wearing sweaters, took them off later, once we were warm. I remember waking in the still heart of the night to hear the distant and unspeakably comforting sound of my father stoking the coal furnace far downstairs in the earthen cellar. Sometimes, between winter storms, sun dogs hung brightly in the west late in the day, flanking the thin luminous sky before sunset. After nightfall the temperature dropped. A cold steady wind rose over the rippled crust of the prairie, carrying with it a fine and quietly hissing powder of driven snow.

SEVEN

(1952)

Hannah

I

I have brought seven books to read during a stay of fourteen days at the lake. This is now the sixth day, and I am halfway through my fourth volume. I do not want to run out of books. Therefore I make an effort to read slowly, putting the book down on my lap between each chapter and gazing for a time out over the blue water.

In this way, I first discover the bears on the lake. Something catches my eye far out on the surface of the water. It is very distant, a small speck that disappears teasingly when I look at it directly. I tilt up the stems of my glasses and peer through the lenses at an angle. I see the speck for a moment, then lose it again in the brightness of scattered sunlight on the moving water.

I lean back in my chaise longue. Idly, I imagine that the speck may be a piece of driftwood, a waterlogged rowboat, perhaps the uprooted stump of a birch carried out in a storm. Then I put these questions out of my mind. I pick up my book. It is *The Master of Ballantrae*, a yellowing volume from my father's bookshelves at home, and the next chapter is entitled "All that Passed on the Night of February 27th, 1757."

When I enter the cottage to get my grandfather's binoculars, my mother and grandmother do not look up from their card game. My grandmother is dealing the cards. As she does so, her cigarette droops from her lips, its smoke curling upward past her squinted eyes. My mother picks up her cards one by one from the red checkered tablecloth, glances at them, then sorts them into her hand. The cottage is silent. Through the door of the front bedroom I can see a corner of the double bed with its light brown spread. On that corner is visible a stockinged foot of my sleeping grandfather. I move across the room toward the empty fireplace, stepping aside to avoid the bearskin hearthrug. I reach up and remove the heavy binoculars from their place on the mantel.

I pause before going back outdoors. Near me is the wooden ladder that goes up the wall beside the stones of the fireplace chimney, leading to the small attic bedroom upstairs. I know that my uncle Charles is in that room, writing a letter at the small pine table overlooking the lake. For a moment or two I choose to remain near him.

"'Good God, madam,' cried I, in a voice not fitting for a sick-room, 'good God, madam, what have you done with my papers?'

"'I have burned them,' said Mrs. Henry, turning about. 'It is enough, it is too much, that you and I have seen them.'

"'This is a fine night's work that you have done!' cried I. 'And all to save the reputation of a man that eat bread by the

shedding of his comrades' blood, as I do by the shedding of
ink.'

"'To save the reputation of that family in which you are
a servant, Mr. Mackellar,' she returned, 'and for which you
have already done so much.'

"'It is a family I will not serve much longer,' I cried, 'for I
am . . .'"

I discover that there are three bears swimming in from the
lake, a mother and two cubs. The binoculars bring them up
close enough so that I can make out their rounded ears, the
low shapes of their heads, which bob with the steady, invisible paddle of their front legs. They are still a great distance
away on the sunlit water. Without the glasses I cannot make
them out distinctly.

I close my book and set it down on the floor of the veranda.
I pull my heels up against the backs of my thighs, and, resting
the binoculars on my raised knees, I peer through the lenses
and watch the bears. I think of telling Malcolm and Ingie,
who are playing on the rocky shore below the cottage. I could
go down and say to them, "Look. Real bears." We could sit
together on the shore and take turns looking through the
binoculars.

But instead I decide that I will not move from the veranda;
I will not alter the moment. I make this decision because I
am convinced that my uncle Charles, sitting at the upstairs
window overlooking the lake, has also seen the bears and is
looking at them at the same moment as I am.

In the calm silence, warmed by the sunlight, I allow myself
to daydream. Images that are derived from the novels I have

been reading take form slowly in my mind, and with a lazy
willingness I make them grow. Jane Austen. Anatole France.
Anton Chekhov. With the ease of dreams, my family and I
appear dressed in the clothing of the early nineteenth century. We are gathered in the front drawing room of a large
cottage, a landowner's manor built of stone at the edge of
a stately forest of Georgian pine. Large windows look out
over a still gray lake. On a draped table stands a steaming
samovar. On another is a decanter of red wine. My father and
grandfather, glasses of wine in their hands, stand at the man-
telpiece, quietly conversing. A small fire of logs burns in the
fireplace behind their knees. In a chair by one window, my
grandmother sits embroidering, an afghan spread over her
lap for warmth. My mother stands at a table and pours tea.
On a patterned carpet, Malcolm and Ingie play a quiet game
of wooden jacks. I am in a window seat at a slight distance
from the rest of the family, gazing out over the surface of the
gray lake. Frail mists play slowly over the mirrorlike water.
Near me is my uncle Charles, standing, his arms folded over
his breast.

In my daydream, the moment is harmonious, quiet, and
serene. As my uncle Charles bends near me, I am somehow secretly aware that the bears are nearing the shore. My
uncle Charles bends closer, his face very near mine. I feel
the sweetness of his breath. He drops to one knee. As he
does so, the bears swim to shore, climb out of the water, and,
unseen by anyone but me, disappear like a blessing of unnoticed symbols into the gray mists of the silent and dripping
forest.

My grandfather comes out onto the veranda in the sunlight. "What have we got here?" he says. I turn in my chaise longue to look at him. In one hand, slung from two hooked fingers, he is carrying his shoes.

"Bears?" says my grandmother. Her face shows disbelief and alarm. She lays her cards on the table and tries to push out her chair. In her hurry, the back legs of the chair become caught in a space between planks on the pine floor. "Help me," she says angrily. Then she calls to my grandfather, "Get the children inside." My grandfather is sitting on the wood-box in the living room, leaning forward tying his shoes, and he does not get up. Freed from her chair, my grandmother strides past him to the veranda door, holds the screen open and shouts out, "Malcolm! Ingie! Come inside right away! There are bears on the lake!" The children look up toward her. Then they glance over their shoulders, as if something might be approaching directly behind them. Suddenly fright-ened, they scramble to their feet and run for the wooden stairs that lead up from the shore.

My mother leans over the veranda railing on the side toward the guest cabin and calls out urgently, "Harold! Harold!" When the door of the guest cabin finally opens and my father comes out, annoyed and impatient at the interrup-tion, he stands on the top step with one hand shielding his eyes, blinking and squinting in the bright light of the sun. His face wears a scowl of angry displeasure.

We cluster on the veranda, watching the bears approach the shore. Malcolm and Ingie lean against the railing, their chins cupped in their hands. My grandmother sits on a straight chair that she has brought out from the dining room table. My mother stands behind her, resting her hands on her mother's shoulders and from time to time kneading the muscles of her neck. My grandfather has mixed himself a drink. He stands behind the rest of us, dissociating himself in a mutely scornful way. Now and then he twirls his drink so that the ice cubes clink against the glass.

None of us knows yet that the bears will be shot. But when at last the exhausted animals reach shore and climb with difficulty onto the rocks, three men appear from inside the edge of the forest, having approached unseen from somewhere farther up the lakefront. As the bears move across the rocks of the shore toward the protection of the forest wall, the men begin shooting. One of them remains upright and fires from a standing position; the two others drop to their knees, like marksmen.

II

Still shots: It is the afternoon of Saturday, August 23rd, 1952. The family has lunched together on fried herring caught in nets from the lake, baking powder biscuits warm from the oven, sliced fresh cucumbers in dill vinegar, red garden tomatoes from the vegetable stand on the highway. Now, following lunch, comes what I consider one of the pleasantest parts of the day—hushed, calm, and still.

The dishes are washed and put away, the linens are folded, the back door has been propped open with a small wedge of pine to let in the warm afternoon air. The members of the family have gone off in their different directions. My grandfather has disappeared into the front bedroom for a nap. My father has gone outdoors to the small guest cabin, where he has taped black oilcloth over the windows to create a dark-room. My mother and grandmother, their chores finished, have settled in at the red checkered tablecloth for a game of canasta. And upstairs, in the small bedroom under the roof, my uncle Charles sits at the window writing a letter.

As for myself, I recline with my book on the front veranda, contented in the heat of the sun that warms the length of my body. I wish to keep this moment from passing; if I were able, I would cling to it eternally. The afternoon is silent, warm, filled with a clear and steady light. The sky is blue and cloudless, the air hushed, the great blue lake immaculately calm. On the rocky shore below the cottage, my brother and sister are catching tadpoles from one of the spring-fed pools that form a loosely connected chain from the wall of the forest down to the edge of the lake. They squat patiently on their haunches, and they are motionless except for the movement of their arms as they draw their punctured tin cans carefully through the shallow water.

Everything around me is still, silent, and calm. It is the perfect time, with my book resting on my lap, to reflect upon the feelings that I am experiencing in my romance with Uncle Charles.

He is not really my uncle. He is the youngest son of my grandmother's youngest brother. He is my grandmother's nephew, my mother's cousin, my own second cousin. But for as long as I can remember, perhaps because of some family joke many years before, he has been called Uncle Charles. He is twenty-nine years old. The last time I saw him was five years earlier, when I myself was eight years old.

He is a soldier. I suspect that this may be part of the reason why my father, unhappy with his own life, so obviously despises him deeply. My father, after all, is already forty-four years old. Having wished for himself a life of travel and high romance, he has allowed himself, by an improbable route that I don't completely understand, to become a chicken farmer on a small farm on the prairie, isolated obscurely in the center of the continent. He has the responsibility of caring not only for a wife but also three children, and even my grandparents, retired now, live there in the winters, when they are not here at the lake, increasing my father's burden and diminishing his freedom by that much more.

In contrast, my uncle Charles is at the pinnacle of his youth and freedom. He is unmarried and has no children. He travels to all parts of the world, carrying the whole of his earthly possessions tucked and folded neatly into a single canvas bag. He goes to war.

I am not certain as to all the details of Uncle Charles' career, but I know its outlines. Like my father, he entered the war in 1942, but at that time Uncle Charles was only nineteen years old. When the war ended, he went to college and afterwards re-entered the army, becoming an officer. He is now a lieutenant. In our few moments together, he has confided in me very little about himself, but he has revealed to the family a certain number of current details: When his visit with us at the lake comes to an end, he will travel by train to an army post in Missouri; after that, he will travel to another post in New Jersey; from there he will be flown to Korea.

Each day after lunch my uncle Charles climbs to the small room under the slant of the roof to write a letter. I imagine myself climbing to the small open hatchway that is the entrance to his room. His back would be toward me. I would find him with his pen poised above the half-filled sheet of paper as he gazes absently through the window, his thoughts wandering. I would wait for a certain length of time, then I would speak his name quietly and watch him turn his face toward mine. I would tell him that I had brought up the glasses, ask if he would please look at the mysterious dark speck on the lake and tell me what it is.

That my uncle Charles is going to war, I admit, intensifies my feelings toward him. But even if he were not going, even if he were not a soldier, I am certain that my love for him would not be diminished. It is Uncle Charles himself that I love. I love his quiet and unassuming manner, his calm politeness, the way he smiles at me on certain occasions, as if speaking to me alone, without words, in such a way that the others won't know of it. I love him for treating me as if I were one of the adults rather than one of the children, for making an effort to include me in the adult conversations at the dinner table, for asking me questions about myself, about school, about my reading. I love him for choosing to come out and stand with me on the veranda in the gathering chill and darkness after dinner, even if only for a few brief minutes, rather than going directly to sit by the fireplace with my grandfather and my father. I love the plainness of his handsome round face. I love the way he stands in front of the fireplace with a glass of whiskey in his hand, modestly, without swaggering (unlike my grandfather), and without seeming that he is trying to tower over the room in silent superiority (unlike my father). I love the plain, hearty look of his thick, ribbed sweater when he pushes the sleeves up onto his tan forearms. I love his hands, which are not large, and I love the tentative, careful, and yet confident way he touches things, as if they were delicate and might easily be harmed—when my grandmother passes him a tureen at the dinner table, when he picks up one of my books and slowly turns its pages, or when Malcolm, in the back yard, offers him his toy balsa wood airplane and asks him to try out its flight.

I have not yet found courage to ask him who it is he writes to in the small upstairs room overlooking the lake.

At last the screen door opens behind me and someone comes onto the veranda where I am sitting alone. I know it is my uncle Charles because he says nothing. Any of the others would have spoken, they would have said something in greeting, would have asked a question.

Instantly, I make my decision, and I continue looking through the binoculars: I will pretend that I do not know he is there. Yet I sense his movements near me. He stands beside the chaise longue; then he lowers himself and drops silently to one knee. He reaches forward and sets a small pair of black field glasses on the wooden railing of the veranda. For balance, he rests one forearm on the arm of the chaise longue, near me. I can feel the warmth of his flesh even though he is not touching me.

Rigid with self-consciousness, I continue looking through the binoculars, pretending foolishly not to know he is there. After a moment he says quietly, "Hannah, those are stronger glasses than mine. Let me take a look."

I hand over the glasses without a word, pausing only to lift the strap over my head. I forget entirely to act surprised.

"I still think they're dangerous," my grandmother says. "We should all be indoors."

Standing behind us with his drink in his hand, my grandfather makes a low, derisive sound, a humorless laugh in his throat. My mother rubs the muscles at the sides of my grandmother's neck to help calm her.

The bears come to shore at a point some distance down the lakefront from our cottage. They are out of sight for a time under the overhang of the shoreline, but then we can see them again as they climb up laboriously over the edge onto the dry rocks. By this time we are all speaking in low, excited whispers. The bears appear exhausted. They move slowly, nudging one another with their snouts, and their bodies seem surprisingly thin and small until they pause to shake the water out of their fur, bringing back some of its fullness. Then they move with a kind of slow rapidity toward the forest edge.

When the bears start moving, the three riflemen appear suddenly from within a copse of birches just behind the guest cabin. They are extremely close to us; I can see their plaid shirts, their wide belts, their leather boots, but they do not even glance in our direction. They run a short distance onto the shore, take their positions, and begin shooting. The first to be killed is one of the cubs. It has lumbered halfway toward the protection of the forest when its front legs collapse underneath it.

On the veranda there is confusion. My grandmother is up from her chair, attempting to usher us all simultaneously back into the safety of the cottage. Malcolm and Ingie are speaking confusedly, with a tone of astonished incredulousness, trying to draw the attention of the adults to what is happening. Ingie begins to cry, tugging at her mother's arm. Around us in the confusion, there is the continuing loud noise of rifle shots. My father has gone inside the cottage, into the coat closet, to put new film into one of his cameras. At precisely this moment he opens the door to come back out onto the veranda, and he is presented with a scene of extreme disorder.

III

The sun warms my body as I recline on the chaise longue. All about me is still, and I observe, merely by turning my head, the visit of a hummingbird, hovering in air, to one of the grandmother's windowboxes of geraniums and petunias nearby. On the shore, Malcolm and Ingie examine tadpoles that they have gathered in a pail. A lone sea gull traverses the shore in silence, level and steady in its flight. Not long after, it is followed by another.

My uncle Charles sits at the front window of the small upstairs bedroom, composing a letter.

"Mr. Henry laid down his cards. He rose to his feet very softly, and seemed all the while like a person in deep thought. 'You coward!' he said, gently, as if to himself. And then, with neither hurry nor any particular violence, he struck the master in the mouth.

"The master sprung to his feet like one transfigured. I had never seen the man so beautiful. 'A blow!' he cried. 'I would not take a blow from God Almighty.'

"'Lower your voice,' said Mr. Henry. 'Do you wish . . .'"

I perceive that my father has been deeply unhappy with the visit of my uncle Charles. There is a stiff and mannered aloofness about him that I recognize as a familiar sign of his displeasure. When he offers Uncle Charles a drink, there is a strained and ungenerous tone in his voice that seems to say, "And I suppose *you* will want a drink, too." At meals he speaks almost not at all and is withdrawn into a chill and arch politeness that does little to make the table more convivial, in spite of the efforts of others.

It is true, as always, that after he has had a number of drinks, my father loosens. During one of the first evenings of the visit, he sat after dinner at the table, with a bottle of wine, and talked with Uncle Charles until almost bedtime about the war. But whatever happens with him in the evenings, in the mornings he is invariably sullen once again, ominously threatening, imperiously stiff and cool. Something in him despises Uncle Charles. During two successive days of the visit, my father decides that he will take long car trips by himself, telling us that he is going for photographs on more northern reaches of the shore, near Split Rock and even farther north toward French River. On one of these occasions he does not return until well after dinnertime has passed and the rest of us have already eaten. At the table that night, eating without him, there is a certain lightness, ease, and frivolity, as if we are having a party. Only my mother seems preoccupied, and frightened.

I think: The room would be warm from sunlight on the roof. There would be the faint, clean scent of pine from the exposed rafters. Poised there, I would be able to hear the frail scratch of his pen on the surface of the paper. I could step silently from the ladder, on very light feet, and stand for a moment at his shoulder . . .

Through my grandfather's binoculars I watch the bears drawing nearer across the blue and imperturbable surface of the lake.

"Hannah, those glasses are stronger than mine. Let me take a look." He is so close to me that I can feel the sweetness of his breath as he whispers the words. And when I give him the glasses, our hands touch for a moment, his fingers gently brushing mine. I pause, not quite releasing the binoculars. I look deeply into his eyes.

"What have we got here?" Frightened, I turn quickly in the chaise longue. My grandfather scowls down at Uncle Charles and me, his face dark and stern. In one hand, hanging down from two hooked fingers, he holds his black shoes.

I can see the riflemen's plaid shirts, their leather boots, the bald spot on one of their heads, but they do not glance in our direction; they are unconcerned about the small crowd of people clustered on our veranda in the sunlight.

At once there is great confusion. My grandmother wants us all back in the cottage. Malcolm and Ingie shout in voices that are astonished and incredulous. Ingie begins to cry, tugging at her mother's arm. Around us, amid the chaos of voices and sudden movement, there is the continuing noise of shots in rapid succession. Sometimes the shots are repeated one almost on top of another; then there is a pause followed abruptly by a new flurry, like a battle.

I hear the sounds and feel the movement as if I were simultaneously close by and a great distance away. I know that I am crying, but it seems to me that I do not in any way feel frightened, and certainly I am not in grief; I understand, in some remote part of myself, that I am crying because in this way I can impress myself more vividly upon my uncle Charles.

There is pleasure, as a result, in my tears, as there is pleasure also, at least for an instant, in what else I have done: quite blindly and yet with a certain quick and heedless decision, I have turned and thrown myself upon my uncle Charles where he stands beside me. I admit that I am amazed at what I have done. But now that this moment has actually come, I make every effort to feel it intensely, and as I imagine it should be felt. I lock my arms tightly around him, I close my eyes, I press my body strenuously against his.

What I feel in the embrace is for a brief moment profound and confusing, but then it is awesomely disappointing: I understand almost at once that I have misjudged, I have made a mistake, I have created an embarrassment. I sense immediately that my uncle Charles is self-conscious, awkward, and wholly without passion in returning my embrace; I feel his hand on one of my arms, pushing me gently but firmly away, and I feel suddenly quite lost; I know that the other adults also will be incredulous and coolly disapproving, that soon I will be more embarrassed even than I am now, and I have no idea what I can possibly do to correct what I have done.

My mind is alert, but of no help. I wish that time would stop, but it does not. I wish I could be saved by my uncle Charles, but I am not. I want all things around me to disappear, but that does not happen either. I am aware that my father has now come out onto the veranda also, compounding the sting of my error, but I determine with a small spark of anger to ignore at least that much of what surrounds me;

I determine to repudiate at least these—my father's piercing anger, his cruel disapproval, his unjust scorn. With this resolve, I seek protection in what is for now, however inadequate, my only place of hiding, and I hold on all the more tightly to my uncle Charles. With my eyes shut and my face buried against him, I cling, and I cling, and I cling, as if for my very life.

IV

After dinner the family, with the exception of my father, sits together in the living room by the dim light of pine logs burning in the fireplace. Nights at the lake are cold; my grandfather will put more logs on the fire before he goes to bed, he will get up once during the night to add more, and in the morning he will use the bellows to bring the fire back to life. By midday the fire will have died, and he will scoop out the cold ash with a small shovel and then sweep the hearth. In the evening, he will light the fire again.

I have realized that I cannot love my uncle Charles, that it is impossible for me to do so. My regret at this knowledge is as intense now as my love was before and far more deeply disheartening.

I say almost nothing all evening, pondering unhappily what has occurred, and wishing earnestly and devoutly to draw no more attention to myself.

My father sits in the dining room at the checkered tablecloth, dismantling and cleaning one of his cameras. The sleeves of his khaki shirt, a remnant from his days in the navy, are rolled up past the elbows. The lamplight shines on his high forehead as he bends over his work. He has removed the lenses of the camera, unscrewed the viewfinder, taken off the barrel and exposed the mechanism of the shutter. With air brushes and small bits of flannel wrapped around toothpicks, he cleans each small piece and every corner.

Malcolm and Ingie are in bed already. When my uncle Charles goes to the wooden ladder to climb upstairs, my father murmurs good night in a toneless voice and neither turns nor looks up from his work.

I lie awake in the darkness until I am certain the adults are all in bed. In the hushed quietness of the cottage I hear sounds that tell me what is happening. I hear footsteps crunching on the gravel path outside my window, then, after a time, returning. I hear the back door being carefully bolted. My grandfather putting logs on the fire. Voices saying good night, the creaking of bedsprings, a pair of shoes being dropped to the floor, a cough. When I am quite certain of the silence, I put on my glasses and, as quietly as I am able, strike a match and light the candle beside my bed.

For a time I do nothing but watch the play of shadows and light on the walls of the room as the candleflame stretches and wavers. Beside me in the bed, Ingie stirs, turns over, falls back asleep with one arm thrown out over the spread. In his cot against the wall, Malcolm sleeps without moving. He is deep under the covers, and I can see no part of him except a scant glimpse of the top of his head.

"It is a strange thing that I should be at a stick for a date—the date, besides, of an incident that changed the very nature of my life, and sent us all into foreign lands. But the truth is that I was stricken out of all my habitudes, and find my journals very ill redd-up, the day not indicated sometimes for a week or two together, and the whole fashion of the thing like that of a man near desperate. It was late March at least, or early April, 1764. I had slept heavily and wakened with a premonition of some evil to befall. So strong was this upon my spirit, that I hurried down stairs in my shirt and breeches, and my hand (I remember) shook upon the rail. It was a cold, sunny morning with a thick white frost; the blackbirds sung exceeding sweet and loud about the house of Durrisdeer, and there was a noise of the sea in all the chambers . . ."

My mother normally would have spoken to me. She would have found some moment when she and I were alone to invite me to confide in her. But in this case I suspect that my father has told her emphatically to say nothing, to let the matter die by itself.

It is strange how this suspicion creates in me a sense of injustice and anger. I wish to be left alone, yet I resent my parents for not coming to my aid.

But of course I must keep silent, however contradictory my feelings might be. From this point on, anything I might say would be misinterpreted by my parents. If I were to tell them that I was deeply in love with my uncle Charles, they could not possibly believe me, thinking me too impressionable and young to know what I was saying. And if I were to tell them that I am no longer in love at all with my uncle Charles, they would be equally unable to believe the truth of what I said, believing that I spoke only in an effort to set them at ease.

I rest my book on my knees. Malcolm and Ingie are soundly asleep. The candle in my hurricane lamp casts a steady and motionless light now on the pine walls of our room. I think of Uncle Charles lying on his narrow cot in the small upstairs room. Perhaps he also is awake, looking into the darkness, or gazing at the faint suggestion of light formed by the window overlooking the lake.

My uncle Charles is going off to war and will soon leave. How easily I could climb the wooden ladder in silence, cross the floor, kneel by his cot. I could so easily explain things to him; he would allow me, he is so kind; he would understand everything, all my apologies, he would understand even when I said that I am no longer in love with him and yet how passionately I want him not to go away.

"The cache of the treasure being hard by, although yet unidentified, it was concluded not to break camp; and the day passed, on the part of the voyagers, in unavailing exploration of the woods, Secundra the while lying on his master's grave . . ."

I do not do this: I do not steal into the living room, cross the soft hearthrug in my bare feet, then climb the wooden ladder, in perfect silence, nothing lighting my way but the dim glow of dying coals inside the screened fireplace. At the top of the ladder I imagine climbing into utter darkness, a blackness so complete that I am blinded entirely and extend one hand uncertainly before me. Quietly I whisper the name Charles; then I do so again, and once again.

In the morning when my uncle Charles leaves, the entire family goes out the back door to stroll along the gravel path and stand beside the car seeing him off. There is the sweet smell of damp cedar in the cold morning air, and the pungent scent of woodsmoke comes thinly from the chimney of the cottage. Rays of morning sunlight penetrate at an angle through the leaves of birches and touch the damp forest floor.

My uncle Charles is wearing his army uniform. He carries his belongings in a green duffle bag, and I watch as he lifts it into the trunk of the car and then stands aside as my father closes down the lid. For a moment the family forms a tableau, but then people step back with the closing of the lid, and it is broken. My uncle Charles shakes my grandfather's hand. He gives Malcolm and Ingie each a kiss on the top of the head. When he comes to me, he hesitates for a brief moment, almost imperceptibly, and then he shakes my hand as well.

After the car disappears around the first bend in the lane, our small group disintegrates. My grandfather excuses himself and walks on the gravel path toward the outhouse. Malcolm and Ingie go down to the shore to look at the lake. My mother and grandmother go into the cottage to have another cup of coffee. After they have drunk their coffee, they dry the breakfast dishes that I have washed. After that they climb the ladder to the small upstairs room and together they change the linens on the bed.

I have nothing to do. For a time I stand at one of the front windows and look out at the lake. Then I sit down at the table. I open a deck of my grandmother's cards, feeling the softness in them that has come with much use. I lay them out in seven rows, and without interest I begin playing.

When he returns from driving my uncle Charles to the station, my father is in the best of spirits, and although I am withdrawn and quiet he makes a show of not noticing.

The morning is so perfect, he says, that he wants to take a walk down the shore for photographs before lunch; I ought to come too. As it turns out, Malcolm and Ingie come as well, following along behind my father and me as we walk down the dirt lane past the first turn, then along the edge of the warm meadow, finally through stands of pine to the outcroppings of rock along the shore. We explore for an hour or two; my father continues to seem unusually happy, as if he is relieved, a nameless and unmentioned burden lifted from him. He takes a full roll of photographs, for which he works very carefully, sometimes kneeling, sometimes lying flat on his stomach, to get angle and light and shadow precisely correct: birch leaves in sunlight, a fisherman's net drying on wooden reels, the oarlock of an abandoned dory, the grain of weathered planking on the side of a fisherman's shed, a delicate pattern of lichen growing on a rock.

My father, as always, is unable to talk to me directly, especially if something intimate or personal might be involved; there is a quality in him that is too intensely self-protective and angrily threatened, too fiercely controlled and held back, too hoarding, too quick to slip over into disapproval, a kind of rough impatience, or anger. I know that he is trying now, but above all without any mention of my departed uncle Charles, to find a way of communicating with me, and I try to respond to his effort with an interest that will seem genuine. But I would rather be elsewhere, I would rather not be with my father just now, and inwardly I find myself feeling angry and increasingly sorry for both of us as he attempts, with his effort at love, to draw me once again into the carefully nurtured and protected capsule of his own world, explaining to me exhaustively what he is doing—talking soberly about shutter

speeds, f-stops, composition, depth of field. Walking toward
home, he picks out still more subjects and quizzes me with
a serious and professorial gravity as to how he should best
shoot them: what speed, aperture, depth of focus for a head
of blossoming clover, a weathered fence post, a stand of birch
in sunlight, an opening vista of the curving shoreline.

When we get back to the cottage, I am not feeling well.
Something is wrong with my vision, which seems to be filled
with pinholes and buzzing with light; my legs are without
weight, my breath is short, and my stomach is very seriously
not right. I excuse myself from lunch and climb deeply under
the covers of my bed.

After two days of rest I am better. Everyone agrees with
relief that I have had an infection, and that once again I am
all right.

V

Still shots: It is the afternoon of Thursday, August 28th,
1952. The family has lunched together on broiled trout
caught from the lake, a loaf of fresh bread warm from the
oven, sliced cucumbers in dill-flavored vinegar, red garden
tomatoes. Now, following lunch, comes the quietest moment
of the day. All things around us are hushed, suspended in
calm. The dishes are done, the linens are folded, the back
door has been propped open with a wedge of pine to let
in the warm afternoon air. My mother and grandmother sit
at the red checkered tablecloth playing a game of canasta.
My grandfather reclines in his easy chair by the empty fireplace, listening to the quiet drone of a baseball game from
somewhere five hundred miles away. My father has locked

himself into the guest cabin to develop film in his darkroom. Malcolm and Ingie are down on the shore, playing a game in which they pretend to see bears swimming in from the lake.

I watch them from the front window of the small upstairs bedroom, the room in which Malcolm is now the one who sleeps at night. I sit at the small pine table, and before me lies the copy of *Emma* that I have just now, lying on Malcolm's bed, finished reading. Next to the closed book is the blank sheet of paper on which at last I intend to capture and send away my feelings. A pen rests on its surface.

From my window, I listen to the distant sounds of Malcolm and Ingie's voices. They sing a brave, lilting refrain as they march back and forth in penguin struts at the edge of the lake. Then, having frightened themselves purposely, they bound and leap like small deer, fleeing over the rocks of the shore to disappear into the edge of the forest. In the wake of their voices, all things are quiet and serene. *My dear Charles*, I begin.

Then I stop. In the writing of them, these few words, with their ludicrous posturing, reveal to me the truth. I am too young; nothing that has happened to me can possibly be taken by others as real. I do not know how, I do not have the means, to explain understandably either the remaining presence of what has happened to me or the loss that I now feel. I have no audience. It will be necessary for me to remain silent.

Slowly I crumple the page. Doing so, I gaze through the window out over the blue expanse of the lake. I see its emptiness, its sun-brightened indifference, the thin blue line of the horizon miles and miles distant.

I get up from my chair, walk over to the narrow bed against the low wall. There I lie down, resting my head on the soft pillow. I am extremely tired. My limbs are unnaturally heavy. I allow my body, bit by bit, to relax into the softness of the mattress beneath me.

The air in the small room is warm from sunlight on the roof of the cottage. From the low, sloping rafters overhead, there comes a faint, clean scent of pine. All around me, as if everywhere, there is stillness and calm.

I dream that three bears are swimming in from the lake. In the manner of all dreams, time and distance behave strangely; the bears swim toward shore for three days, visible far out on the motionless lake. When I am inside the dream, I know somehow that my uncle Charles has died; but I am aware that I have not yet learned of his death. From the bed I watch myself sitting at the window in the small upstairs room, looking out over the lake.

I learn of the bears when I return from a walk to the highway, where I have gone to bring in the mail. At the highway, I find no mail; peering into the wooden box, shaped like a miniature cottage, I see only a small scene of rolling hills, flocks of small sheep grazing quietly on green grass. I am surprised but not surprised; in all things around me there seems to be a luxuriant, poised calm, warmed by sunlight. On my return to the cottage, I find Malcolm and Ingie flying a toy balsa wood airplane in the backyard.

"Hannah," Malcolm tells me, "there are bears on the lake." He launches the plane from his cocked arm and it rises on the warm air, its wings quivering slightly; then it descends toward Ingie standing on the far side of the lawn against the dark wall of the forest.

"Oooooh," Ingie croons, extending her hands. "Come, little airplane."

I go into the cottage through the open kitchen door. My grandmother is taking corn muffins from the oven. Her wide back is toward me. "Lunchtime," she says without looking at me. "Call the children."

"I am one of the children," I tell her.

"Call the children," she says, but I realize that she is no longer speaking to me, but to someone else, whom I cannot see.

In the dining room, my mother sets a platter of fried herring on the table. It is garnished with parsley and wedges of lemon. Then time slips away from me and there are no herring and the table is empty. As usual in the dream, there is a drifting silence that moves around me like silent, rustling snow. In the living room, my grandfather sits alone by the empty fireplace dressed in a dark pin-striped suit with a buttoned vest. He is dressed impeccably, with gleaming black shoes and stiff white cuffs that show at his wrists. In one hand he holds a glass of whiskey.

"Where is my father?" I ask him.

"Your father is in his darkroom," he says.

"And Uncle Charles?"

"Your uncle Charles is writing a letter."

I ask him: "Have you seen the bears?"

My grandfather sips from his whiskey. He purses his lips against the strength of the liquor. "I have not seen the bears," he says. "I know nothing of the bears. The bears do not exist."

My uncle Charles comes in and out of the dream. I climb the wooden ladder to the small upstairs room and find him sitting at the window overlooking the lake. He is writing a letter. My uncle Charles is young, modest, kind, and poised; I am devoted in my belief that I love him deeply. I am thirteen years old, and for me he is a figure of romance; he is youth and freedom, he is my belief in the past, and he is the energy that will sweep me into the future.

I sit on the edge of the table. It is so quiet in the room that I can hear the frail scratch of his pen as he writes.

When he looks up at me, I say to him: "Dear Charles, I don't want you to die." I am aware that I am being an actress, that I am attempting coolly to imitate a voice that has come to me from the novels I have read. And yet in spite of this awareness of falsehood, I find myself struggling not to weep.

My uncle Charles smiles at me, laughs kindly. He meets my eyes and covers one of my hands with his. At this moment I love him wholly, I will love him forever. "Hannah," he says to me, gently, "you're only dreaming."

My uncle Charles is gone and I sit at the window of the small upstairs room, overlooking the lake. I am holding an old copy of *Emma*, and on the smooth surface of the lake I see three bears swimming toward shore from the far distance, but they seem not to be moving.

My father is celebrating his birthday. It is night. The stems of the wine glasses have been broken off, and we sit in chairs around the table, holding them upright with our hands. Under the lamplight, my father's high brow is sweating. He announces: "My antipathy toward Uncle Charles has dissipated." He grimaces with pain and tears viciously at one fingernail with his bared teeth. My grandmother rises from the table, letting her wine glass tip onto the checkered cloth.

A fan of dark wine spreads outward under the lamplight. Unconcerned, my grandmother shakes flea powder on the large white cat as it walks slowly through the doorway into the kitchen.

I know that my dream lasts three days, although the days are not clearly marked. My father has taped black oilcloth over the windows of the guest cabin, blinding them. Malcolm finds a toad at the edge of the forest and bursts open the door to show my father. As sunlight strikes my father in the back, his arms shoot up over his head and he screams in pain and anger. Malcolm flees to find a hiding place under the cottage, dropping the toad on the darkroom floor. My uncle Charles is upstairs in the small room, writing a letter.

On the second night my grandmother opens a door in the living room, and inside it is a slot machine. My grandfather, scowling, gives Malcolm and Ingie nickels to play the machine. They pull down the arm, spinning stars and lemons. I hear the *thrush* of coins rushing into the jackpot, and gradually, as if gathering slowly from a distance, that sound becomes the sound of weeping. I perceive slowly that the weeping is my own, and I step from the living room into my bedroom and see myself lying on my bed crying.

I am lying in my bed reading by the light of a candle. My uncle Charles comes to the door of my room, dressed in his army uniform. The rest of the house is asleep.

"Hannah," he whispers. "I must go now."

I am dressed only in my nightgown, and my uncle Charles carries me in his arms out of the cottage and down onto the shore of the lake. He kisses me on the forehead, then steps into a small wooden boat and rows on a diagonal course toward the distant, invisible horizon. In only an instant he is plucked from me, miles away, gone from sight.

I hear my grandfather's voice. I turn toward it and see him hold out a thin-stemmed goblet.

He says, "Brandy, Charles?"

I am there, watching. My mother is playing a spinet in one corner of the room. My grandmother sits in a rocking chair, a piece of embroidery on her lap. Logs crackle quietly in the fireplace and my father and my uncle Charles stand near the warmth of the flames as my grandfather hands them glasses of brandy. Malcolm and Ingie, dressed in clothing of the eighteenth century, play wooden jacks on the floor.

"Prosit," says my father.

"Health," says my grandfather.

"To the long life of the republic," says my uncle Charles, radiant with youth, poise, a quiet confidence. The three of them touch glasses. My mother continues to play the harpsichord, my grandmother to embroider. I am aware that in the darkness outside the windows the bears are at last climbing from the water onto the rocks of the shore. As they lumber toward safety they are killed by the fire from artillery emplacements that have been built with perfect naturalness into the edge of the forest. The destruction of the bears occurs in silence. No one in the room takes notice as the animals, their bodies illuminated by flashes of white light from the guns, writhe grotesquely, throw their great paws upward against the sky. I run toward a window to look out, but I am met there by a face pressed close to the other side. It is the face of a flier. He wears a gas mask, and no flesh is visible on his face. The lenses of his goggles are opaque. A black hose comes out of his insect mouth. I move quickly, gasping in terror, back from the window toward where my uncle Charles is standing by the fireplace, to pull at his arm, but when I touch him there is nothing there, and then I realize that it is only a dream, that it is still the night before, the bears are still swimming in from the lake, I am in my nightgown on the shore, and my uncle Charles is moving rapidly, in his wooden boat, toward the dark horizon. In the calm silence of the night I can hear the breathing of the bears as they come closer and closer, their breath deep and rasping and hollow.

I awake later from my dream. I am standing with a letter in my hand. Malcolm and Ingie are flying a toy airplane in sunlight somewhere in a flowered meadow. "Lunchtime," my grandmother says, her back toward me. The white cat springs silently to a windowsill, raises one paw and begins licking it. In the living room my grandfather is standing alone in front of the empty fireplace, a glass of whiskey in his hand. He is scowling. But then he sets his glass on the mantel and turns toward me where I stand in the doorway. He opens his arms and I move toward him across the room. Somehow the letter is now in his hand; it is open and I know it has been read. My grandfather is weeping, his face is dissolving in grief, it is a painting streaked and disappearing under rain. I move closer. His arms are hollow and thin and light as he embraces me, a skeleton's ancient bones. "Hannah," he whispers, his voice distant, rustling, and small, like thin snow drifting in winter, "this letter has come, it's for you."

NOTEBOOK

I realize now that, throughout my own boyhood, what my father's silence meant to me was this: When he was my age, when he was the way I am now, my father had not existed. Therefore I did not exist either.

EIGHT

(1955)

It was the low narrow attic over the kitchen that became my last refuge before I left home altogether. Only at its exact center, directly under the ridgepole, could I stand up to the full extent of my height without bruising my head on rafters or roof boards, but this was a limitation of no great importance, since by choice I spent most of my time sitting, or even lying, down, unconcerned by the rich carpet of dust that, at least at the beginning, coated the boards beneath me like a kind of soft snow.

At the far end of the attic was set a lone window, hexagonal in shape, the inside of whose panes I took great care to free of cobwebs and dust with my handkerchief. Here was my only source of light. Near the window rose the red brick chimney that began its ascent in the house's earthen basement and completed its climb by projecting through the ridgepole above me into the open air. The proximity of window and chimney was one of the fine treasures of the attic; they were so convenient to one another that, sitting down, I could gaze out of the one while leaning my back comfortably against the other. Indeed, I did so for hours, days, even weeks and

months (if taken all together) of that part of my life: my feet
placed against the outside edges of the window, in the manner of an aircraft gunner, I would sit with my back pressed
firmly against the old red bricks of the chimney behind me.
It was as though (I fancied) I were the pilot of the house,
guiding it through turbulent air, the lookout nested in the
top of its mainmast, or its guardian spirit floating like a car-
penter's bubble in the very peak of its gable, my form dimly
visible from the outside to any who cared to look carefully
enough.

The furnishings of the attic were spare, although without
doubt they grew to have their importance to me, with the
exception only of the broken Christmas ornaments, a jum-
bled collection in a woebegone and collapsing box in one of
the deep corners. Even with these I once began to decorate
the rough rafters of the attic, hanging broken glass balls and
tarnished silver festoons, until, thinking better of it, I retired
them again to their dusty corner. Nothing else remained for
my discovery but the two trunks and the antiquated mirror.
The mirror was an oval piece in a wooden frame of cracked
varnish left behind, I imagined, by some previous resident of
the farmhouse while all else was carried on by creaking wagon
to the next destination westward—Wheatland, New Prague,
Rush River, Sacred Heart. Abandoned, it stood alone and
slightly cockeyed against the sloping rafters of the old attic.
Even so, over the interminable months, its murky, tarnished
surface, with which I became so deeply familiar, stirred
something reverberant within me and gave me occasion as
often as not to lower my trousers and masturbate. Thus I
would admire my stiffened organ in its dim historic surface,
which I was certain had seen countless others identical to it

in time—stark and upright in the grip of the hand, like mine, being touched among thick patchwork quilts in the light of a still candle, or thrusting hurriedly between the ivory-pale legs of women in voluminous white petticoats and hook-eye boots. My own solitary and ungenerative seed, in the mirror's image, again and again I ejaculated through the dead air and into the thick dust of the attic floor, where it fell in heavy, quiet globs like the first drops of rain in the dust of dry fields, leading me idly to wonder whether in the dark of night small mice would tentatively feed on its substance, or spiders come forth to drink it.

All else that remained in the attic were the two trunks, in which lay the remnants of my father. Here indeed I came upon my true heritage, and I approached the discovery with great care, for quite suddenly I had reason to hope for answers to the questions that otherwise eluded me so entirely. I studied the trunks coolly, examined them carefully, like a rodent searching for a nest. As chance would have it, I explored first the older of the two, the small wooden sea trunk with its domed top, saving for later the metal foot locker painted in worn olive drab.

As I removed the articles one after another I placed them carefully in a pattern around me that would enable me, if I chose, to replace them in precisely the reverse order from that in which I first took them out. Even now I remember them exactly:

1 Inside the dome, squatting like a large
   insect, lay a brown lacquered model
   of a World War I biplane;
2 beneath the biplane were folded a boy's

pair of knickers, two argyle knee socks,
a shirt with a square blue collar like a
sailor's blouse;

3 below the knickers, a wooden tennis
racket, its gut strings broken, sprung,
and tangled;

4 a pair of pleated white flannel trousers
and a dark blue sport coat (double
breasted with six brass buttons);

5 a fountain pen of horn;

6 two journal books with marbled covers,
closely handwritten with lecture notes;

7 six briar pipes, charcoaled inside the
bowls and bitten at the stems;

8 a heavy leather trench coat, cracking from
neglect and age, and occupying by itself a
third of the trunk's space;

9 a copy of *Rasselas*, by Samuel Johnson;

10 *Wolf Solent*, by John Cowper Powys;

11 *The Young Carthaginian*, by G. A. Henty;

12 *The Boy Scout Manual*, dated 1918;

13 a highway map of New Jersey, dated 1921;

14 a pocket compass;

15 a map of Yosemite National Park;

16 a Latin primer published in 1913 in
Albany, New York;

17 a phonograph record of Bix Beiderbeck
and the Wolverines playing "Davenport
Blues";

18 a fishing reel without rod or line;

19 a waterproof match holder with three
wooden matches that rattled inside;

20 a pocket flask with leather cover;
21 a corkscrew;
22 a magnifying glass, also with a leather
    cover;
23 an English Queen Victoria penny, dated
    1898;
24 an agate (cut but not polished);
25 a chestnut on a long string;
26 a Yale key of brass, which did not fit the
    lock of the trunk (which was not, in any
    case, locked).

Such were the glimpses of my father that I arranged in expanding circles on the dusty floor of the attic around me. For a week or two I sat in their midst. Perhaps at last I was making progress, yet my impression remained still one of confusion and vagueness, in spite of the detailed concreteness of these objects from the trunk. In what order, after all, was I to take them as representations of the stages of my father's life—about which he himself so seldom begrudged even a word? Was there a chronology to them, other, for example, than the order in which they were layered into the trunk? Were they, for that matter, his, indisputably connected with him? Sitting cross-legged on the attic floor, I asked the questions that my logic told me were as close as I could come, without other help, to the truth:

1 Had my father worn a heavy leather
   trench coat?
2 Had he sported a dark blue jacket with six
   brass buttons; white flannel trousers?
3 Had he traveled the highways of New
   Jersey?

4 Had he attended lectures, been a Boy
   Scout, learned Latin?
5 Had he listened to "Davenport Blues"?
6 Had he used a pocket compass?
7 Had he played tennis with gut strings?
8 Had he struck matches?
9 Had he fished?
10 Where?
11 When?
12 Etc.

It was true that I possessed evidence of a number of things, surrounding me in the silent dust of the attic, but did I have proof really of anything? What, even now, was I to believe? And upon what was I to base my beliefs? What sense was I to make of my father out of these alleged glimpses of him, thin cracks in the varnish of time, which, for all their seeming concreteness, left him practically speaking still an abstraction—or, at best, still failed to explain him as I knew him, as the sullen, dangerous, threatening figure whom I could sense late each afternoon moving nervously through the echoing rooms of the empty house below me, slamming doors as darkness settled in and the plummeting cold outdoors made the old house begin to shrink and creak? What relationship was there between my father in pleated white trousers and my father in barnyard boots kicking the kitchen door off its hinges? Between my father with a chestnut on a long string and my father staring scornfully at me during breakfast and shaming me into terror? Between my father on the highways of New Jersey in 1921 and my father cursing and pacing the rooms, entrapped and sullen, of the empty house below me?

Not desperately, but because it remained to be done, I

turned to the metal foot locker and proceeded with it precisely as I had earlier with the small wooden sea trunk. Among the contents, I rapidly perceived, was greater coherence. Here I came not upon a span of history, but a nugget. Here was focus. I withdrew from the locker:

1 A white naval officer's uniform (with white shoes);

2 a blue naval officer's uniform (with black shoes);

3 a khaki naval officer's uniform (with no shoes);

4 a folded map of the Pacific Ocean that had straight lines drawn in many directions and with great variety across its light blue surface, indicating, I assumed, voyages;

5 a small packet of Japanese currency, rolled up tightly and inserted into

6 the empty brass casing of a large artillery shell, approximately eight inches in length;

7 three clips of brass rifle shells, their ends tapered to a graceful sharpness;

8 a combat helmet, with decayed leather chin strap;

9 a short, stubby bayonet, heavy in the hand, and covered with something faintly grainy, that I could perceive only to be a thin layer of aged, rancid oil;

10 three miniature black elephants of heavy metal, their tusks tipped in smooth white ivory, capable of being arranged in such

a manner that the extended trunk of each
touched the curled tail of another.

•

Thus I possessed, in spiraling circles on the attic floor
around me, the raw materials for a perception of my father—
this man who had, after all, in spite of the little I truly knew of
him, influenced my life so noticeably. It was several months,
the length certainly of a winter, before I packed them away
again. In the meantime I immersed myself in them, imagining that by experiencing through them those same things my
father himself had experienced, I might come at last upon
an understanding of him. In the beginning I devoted a day's
work to each of the artifacts, holding them in my hands and
studying them carefully from every angle as I sat facing the
window, my back leaning comfortably against the chimney:
one day for a close study of the brass key, for example, one
day for the unpolished agate, one for each of the maps, a day
for the corkscrew, one for the tennis racket, a day for the
chestnut, one for the bayonet, another for the match holder,
one for the elephants, a day for the fishing reel, one for the
combat helmet, and so on. The calendar of my life became
the calendar of these historical objects. Finishing with them,
I went on to the written documents: *Rasselas*, the handwritten lecture notes (on mechanical physics, the English lit-
erature of the Augustan Age, the comedies of Shakespeare),
The Boy Scout Manual, *The Young Carthaginian*, etc. After
these (it was, I imagine, near the end of February), I went
one step further, devoting a single day to the wearing of each
of the different suits of clothing. I would get, if possible,
inside my father. The only suit, however, that fit me properly
was the first I had discovered, the one made up of knickers,

argyle knee socks, and the blue sailor blouse with its large square collar. I wore it, sitting again for the length of a day by the window, gazing out at the barren treacheries of the neglected and snow-filled farmyard below. Then followed the others, day by day, a sequence of costumes each of which it was necessary to roll up a foot or so at the cuffs and six or eight inches in the sleeves: the naval uniforms, the flannel trousers and blue jacket, finally the heavy, cracking trench coat, which posed a special problem, since it could not with ease be rolled up at the bottom, and in which, I remember, I fell asleep at the window.

·

My falling asleep was not without meaning. I saw in it an indication that I was failing to progress in my search as I had hoped I would, that my project was not, after all, working in a way wholly satisfactory. After a day's thought, I decided that the trouble lay in my failure to approach the contents of the two trunks in a manner sufficiently organic: I was studying each of the pieces separately rather than identifying the multitudinous connections and relationships that must have existed between them, making up, more accurately, the true experience of my father's past. Therefore I embarked upon a new method of experimentation altogether. I grouped the items and artifacts in a number of changing combinations in the hopes of stumbling upon the key to their subtle and more truly historic nature. If I was lucky, I would find at last not merely dead artifacts, but the living history of my father himself.

I persevered. One day I would dress in the khaki naval officer's uniform, place in one pocket the leather flask, in another the Latin primer and the Queen Victoria penny, then sit at the window studying *The Boy Scout Manual* or the map of Yosemite Park. Another day I would dress in the flannel trousers and blue blazer, filling the pockets with the three elephants, the artillery shell, and the empty fishing reel, then sit studying the map of the Pacific Ocean or reading the lecture notes on Shakespeare's comedies and perhaps, between pages, fondling the World War I biplane. Or I would dress in the knickers and argyle socks and sailor blouse, place on my head the combat helmet, fill my pockets with the six briar pipes, the corkscrew, the rifle clips and the Japanese currency and study the map of the highways of New Jersey.

Altogether, it accomplished little. After a month or so of studying combinations of every possible kind and waiting fruitlessly for a new understanding to come, I resigned myself to failure and determined finally to replace the objects in the two trunks in precisely the reverse order from which, so long ago, I had taken them out. But in doing so, I came upon one last piece of evidence, which altered everything. Inside the locker was a small hidden pocket, hardly visible, which I had overlooked entirely. In it I discovered a packet of seventeen old photographs, cracked, much handled, and well worn, every one of them a picture of none other than my father himself. That he may have been vain had not occurred to me previously; but neither was that thought foremost in my awareness just then. For here I had stumbled upon the one bit of evidence, unexpected but also undeniable, proving that at least once in his life my father had been thoroughly, unquestionably, happy.

At first I was deeply puzzled, for here was represented a man I had never before known even to exist; yet the more I pondered the matter the more it began at last to make things clear: I began gradually to feel that perhaps I had accomplished my task after all. After several days of close study at the window, I concluded that at last I had found him; here was my father.

The discovery, now that I had made it, surprised me most of all by the absence of joy it brought me; perhaps I had found my father, but I perceived quickly as well that I had found no good reason to expect that he would ever come closer to me in his present life. Here, after all, I saw photo after photo of my father as he had never before revealed himself even faintly to me: a man young, dashing, and handsome, with trim groomed mustache, black luxuriant hair, and, invariably, an expression of amusement, contentedness with himself, and easy happiness.

Why should I suddenly hope to know this man when I had never known him before? Why should I suddenly hope now that he might open himself to me when he had never done so before? Here, in one small, cracked photograph after another, was a father I had never known. Here was my father at the rail of a ship at sea, the wind lifting the point of his immaculate collar. Here was my father in the prow of a small boat on rather large swells, smiling back at the camera, his shirt open at the neck. My father at the wheel of a ship; under a spreading palm tree; leaning with a raised arm against the tip of an airplane wing. Standing with his arm around a companion officer on a vast white beach, surf rolling onto the sand in the background. My father always smiling, happy, content with himself. My father always crisp, always fresh, adventurous, and always young: my father sitting at a small round table in an outdoor cafe, under palm leaves, smiling coyly, his hands clasped as if in prayer over a glass of whiskey, while around the base of the glass (connecting my father at last and indisputably with the artifacts I had come upon in the attic) stand three small black elephants, their tusks tipped in smooth white ivory, the trunk of each touching the curled tail of another.

·

Not long after this I abandoned the attic; things in my life began rapidly to change. I came to fear that my father might suspect my presence above his head, although it was true that until then he had shown no signs of suspicion. Perhaps equally important, my grandfather had arrived at last, coming to keep order, and I perceived that it was not impossible that he might search me out himself and beat me from the attic out into the open with his stick. I had learned already how determined my aging and organizational grandfather could be, and it was at this point, quite secretly, that I moved out of the house altogether and took up living in the tin cupola on the ridgepole of the barn.

As for the photographs, it was true that they prepared me, to a slight degree at least, for the beginning of my father's final drawing away from me. Yet still it was painful, as aspects of growing up can always be painful. I make no complaint. I regret only that nothing else had prepared me for it. No hint was given, I had no idea when to expect it, or whether, for that matter, to expect anything at all.

It happened during the silent part of a summer afternoon, that hushed time in the heart of the day when everything seems to be asleep. My father and grandfather had spent the morning inside the old farmhouse together, and at last, as I peered out through one of the jagged old bullet holes in the tin of my cupola (to which, most of the time, I kept an eye pressed), I saw my grandfather come out onto the low west porch and take his customary seat, his hands resting comfortably, one atop the other, on the silver head of his slender walking stick. He sat that way for what seemed hours, not moving. Everything from horizon to horizon was suspended in silence. The pigeons nesting in the cupola around me stirred occasionally, ruffled their feathers, fell back to sleep. The air all around me was still, silent, and warm. Perhaps I myself slept, forehead against the tin. Then I was startled by a crash from the direction of the farmhouse, and I opened my eyes to see that the hexagonal window at the end of the attic had burst outward. Through it came the ancient oval mirror, glinting once in the sun as it turned, then curving down the height of the house to the ground, where with a second, yet muffled, crash, it broke into a thousand pieces and lay hidden in the tall and uncropped summer grass.

My father, then, had at last entered the attic, and with a certain calm practicality I considered for a moment my good fortune in not having been there myself to be greeted by him. Other considerations occurred to me, mainly in the form of questions, and all of them briefly (what was he doing there? what did it mean? and why had he chosen to throw out only the mirror, before whose dim, receding, and richly historic face so much of my own life, some of its most memorable moments, at that, had been lived?). But quickly I set these ruminations aside, moved them to the back of my mind in the acquiescent and pragmatic manner which had become so familiar and representative a trait of my character. Answers to such questions, in any case, were not likely to be forthcoming. As for the immediate scene playing itself out before me, what seemed an inordinate length of time passed between the crash of the mirror to the ground and any subsequent sound or sign of movement. The thing seemed without result,

swallowed into a hole of time. Yet I waited, in silence, and
at last the side door of the old house opened downstairs and
my father emerged. He was dressed, to my great surprise,
in his spotless white naval officer's uniform, and he dragged
behind him, gripping them by the handles, one in each hand,
the small wooden sea chest and the olive drab locker. On
the west porch my grandfather did not once move, did not
even turn his head. Nor did my father so much as glance in
my grandfather's direction, let alone in mine. Brilliant with
whiteness, he simply moved away from the house in an absolutely straight line, never once pausing: across a corner of
the shaded lawn beneath the trees, across the unused gravel
road, through the weed-choked drainage ditch, then diago-
nally across a vast field of ripening wheat, trudging southwest
in the bright sunlight, leaving behind him a trail of bent grain
where he dragged the two trunks.

He came to the peak of the first low hill, disappeared
into the small valley behind it, then reappeared, achingly
white, on the next crest, a smaller figure than before but with
precisely the same determined posture, moving at precisely
the same speed and in precisely the same direction. Nothing else in the universe moved: only my father. From my
cupola I watched him rise slowly to the peak of hill after hill,
diminishing gradually into the distance, until he was merely
a bright white speck in the sunlight, and then, crossing over
the horizon at last, nothing at all.

From the cupola, I watched that small spot on the horizon
until my eyes ached and blurred and at last my vision swam
and failed me. That was it, then; it was over. He was gone;
he had left me: I was alone.

NOTEBOOK

Children, before they are born, are a part of history; after they are born, they are at its mercy.

NINE
(1907–1958)

Early each morning, Peter Thunberg went out to tend the herring nets; in the gray hush of dawn I would wake up to hear the frail, wavering drone of the outboard motor on the lake. It was a sound that never failed to appeal to me strongly. Often during that last of so many visits, I indulged in the fantasy of myself as a prisoner, held in the service of my aging grandfather, and I imagined that the sound of the small fisherman's boat suggested images of escape and romance.

After listening for a time, I would force myself to climb from the warmth of my bed and walk over the cold wooden floor, past the open packing boxes and the remaining pieces of furniture draped with sheets, to one of the front windows of the cottage. There, as my breath clouded the pane, I would watch the boat moving slowly outward across the calm surface of the water. Behind it lay a smooth and silent wake, gently widening, like opening arms.

It was a scene composed entirely in shades of gray. Banks and layers of early-morning fog hung suspended over the smooth water, and the pale skiff moved in and out among them, at times disappearing entirely from my view.

I would dress in silence, listening carefully for sounds of my grandfather's waking in the adjoining room. Stealing out past the emptied cabinets in the kitchen, I would draw the stiff pine door behind me until I heard the faint click of its falling latch, and then I would set out on the narrow dirt road that made its way along the edge of the forest facing the lake. I walked past tiny log cabins with curtains drawn tightly over their windows. Cars covered with beaded dew were parked in the long grass off the edge of the road or stood nosed against the small cabins with vacant eyes, like nuzzling beasts. If I stopped walking, I could hear the faint drone of the outboard motor far up the shore, and then its sudden absence as Peter Thunberg turned off the motor and let the boat drift into place alongside the nets.

A lone sea gull, then another, flew in graceful silence along the rocky shore. I watched the red sun, engorged and flattened into an oval, glide upward from beneath the far rim of the earth. Touched by its sudden light, stands of birch trees along the road beside me turned first red, then silver. Shoals of brightened fog rose slowly, like stage curtains, from the surface of the lake.

·

My grandmother died of a stopped heart late one night, in our farmhouse, in November of 1956. Overweight, short of breath, her arteries clogged with fat, she had been warned by the doctor to change her habits, to drink less whiskey, not eat fried foods, do without butter and salt, stop smoking cigarettes. She refused to believe the things he told her, or could not bear to, and she went on living as she had lived before, ridiculing the idea that she was dancing with death. When it did come, her end was sudden and sadly undramatic.

Sometime near two o'clock in the morning, she awoke with a sharp pain in her back; she declared it to be, as she always did at that time in her life, a pulled muscle. Under the pressure of my grandfather's massaging hands, she stiffened, struggled horribly for some moments like a gasping fish, and died.

.

In her youth, under the influence of her schoolteacher Rebecca Kerndon, my grandmother came to believe that she possessed a calling to become an actress on the stage. Rebecca Kerndon, a young and attractive woman who appreciated the classics of the drama and who frequently read lyric poetry and passages from dramatic texts aloud to her students, instilled in my grandmother, early on, a romantic idea about the stage and the calling of those who appeared magically upon it. But the nature of my grandmother's character was such as to limit the further extent or growth of this influence, and Rebecca Kerndon was unable to turn my grandmother, for example, in a more literary or studious direction, or to cause her to form the habit of seeking out and reading on her own the novels and plays from which the roles she admired were drawn.

As her life went on, my grandmother did not develop in learning, taste, or discrimination, but the energy of her early infatuation stayed with her and made of her an effective imitator, particularly of things she saw on the movie screen. She was capable, in her early adult years, of being passionately histrionic when she wished. In those years also she possessed and made use of a volatile and at times a truly fiery temper. She developed, further, as a means of asserting and defining herself, a number of flamboyant personal habits. She affected the use of a long cigarette holder made of ebony and polished ivory. She wore large ornate brooches to heighten the effect of deep décolletage in the dresses she chose to wear. She familiarized herself with all manner of card games and for a time became known as a daring and expert gambler in certain private circles. Both in private gatherings and at public bars she drew attention to herself by requesting her whiskey in shotglasses, neat. Perhaps most important to those closest to her, she became adept, in the tradition of a certain type of romantic heroine, at dramatizing and simultaneously denying the pain and intense suffering caused her by a variety of physical and emotional ailments that, as it happened, pursued her throughout her life.

·

The sun was half an hour above the horizon, and a morning breeze had risen over the lake. It teased the surface of the lake into gray-blue patches, then crossed the pebble beach where I stood at the water's edge and moved through the shimmering silver birches on the ascent behind me.

Far out over the water, nearly invisible on the thin blue edge of the horizon, lay the ore boats bound outward from Duluth and Two Harbors, steaming slowly uplake toward the locks at Sault Sainte Marie. Smoke from their funnels drifted thinly behind them. Often at night in the earlier years I watched their glimmering lights from behind the windows of the warm cottage, or looked through my grandfather's heavy binoculars to bring them closer over the open miles of dark cold water. There were tales of old wrecks lying undisturbed on the rocky bottom near Castle Danger, Split Rock, French River. In the long evenings it was quiet in the cottage after dinner, my grandfather smoking his cigar by the fire, my grandmother playing cards by lamplight on the red-checkered tablecloth. Some nights there were fog and deep silence all around us, water dripping quietly from the limbs of trees onto the forest floor.

.

Asthma accompanied my grandmother throughout much of her life. It made its first appearance in 1908, after the birth of her daughter, then remained quiescent for a large number of years. In 1931 it reappeared. The ailment was worse during the summer months, and for relief my grandparents began, in the year 1933, spending much of each summer on the shore of Lake Superior, leaving the movie theater in West Tree either dark or in the hands of my father, its assistant manager. Season by season, as they grew older, they became increasingly fond of the quiet pleasures afforded by the lake and grew to think of it as an extended part of their home. In 1938 they bought their own cottage, by this time having become an aging couple married more than thirty years, their roots far in the past, themselves already history.

.

The tall, quietly genteel old man by the name of Kelly, himself past his seventieth year, was one of their oldest friends, going back to what I thought of as the very beginning, a time that for me remained veiled inevitably in faded archaism and awkward romance. Unlike my grandfather, who had never been a soldier, Kelly had fought in the First World War, in France, where as an officer he was gassed and hit by shrapnel so that he breathed with one damaged lung and had a slight, barely noticeable limp when he walked. There was a persistent tale, having become over the years vague and greatly obscured, of an early and romantic episode between my grandmother and Kelly, causing high passion and the display of great jealousy in the family. When on occasion, many decades later, he came to play cards at the lake with my grandparents, I observed his fine white hair, his high forehead and bushy white eyebrows, and his hands with their slender long fingers. I thought of Verdun, Belleau Wood, tarnished metal long since abandoned, antique leather, and I imagined a small group of men on horseback in early morning mist, standing motionlessly, surveying cratered earth.

．

One day in 1921, when she was thirteen years old and in the eighth grade, my mother came home from school to discover, in the front room, my grandfather aiming a pistol at my grandmother's heart. It was the occasion of only one of their many quarrels of sexual jealousy and confused passion, but I believe it was scenes such as these that had the peculiar effect of causing their introverted young daughter to feel that she must, whatever else, devote her life to the protection of her parents.

Certainly my mother was frightened by their passion and rage, especially since these were turned at times even against her. But in addition to her fear I believe that she was poignantly embarrassed for her parents—the poor illiteracy of their thwarted passions that found expression only in the crude artificialities of bombast; their postures and gesturings that were inherited clumsily and in derelict phrases from the bathos and excesses of the old-fashioned stage.

That day after school, her enraged, grim, and scowling father stood squarely in the center of the fringed carpet, his legs spread wide, one arm extended straight out before him, terminating with the steadied pistol in his hand. Her mother sat on the edge of a horsehair love seat, her clothing disheveled, tears streaking her face. Her arms were spread wide, and through her tears, a trembling hysteria in her voice, she brought down imprecations upon the unfeeling breast of her despised and callous husband, urging and daring him to bring an end at once to her worthless and derided life.

.

Sometimes in the afternoons I would follow the dirt road through the forest to where the great meadow opened out, carrying with me a small pail for strawberries. In the meadow the grasses were tall, and my figure would be hidden as I kneeled down and searched for berries underneath the green leaves of the plants. The afternoon air was quiet and still as I worked, and the sun warmed my body.

One afternoon when I stood up to stretch my legs I caught sight of a figure moving on the far side of the meadow against the dark wall of the forest. I shaded my eyes with one hand and saw that it was Kelly, hiking around the perimeter of the meadow. He wore a white sun helmet and carried a long stick as he walked. He seemed to move with an intent kind of determination, walking rather quickly, with his head bowed slightly forward.

I shouted out and the old man stopped abruptly. He looked one way and then another across the meadow, seeking in vain to find me where I stood. I waved an arm over my head in greeting, then did so again, and still again. Perhaps he could not see me in the glare of the sunlight. He stood for some time, shading his eyes with one hand, peering vaguely in my direction through the small round lenses of his glasses. I saw that the white helmet rested slightly askew on his head, tilting off a little oddly to one side. The time that we stood poised in this way seemed to me of a considerable length.

But before I could determine whether to call out again, he turned suddenly and continued his walk, moving in the sunlight against the forest wall with the same intent pace as before, his head studiously bowed, his stick moving mechanically at his side. I watched him for some time, until, coming upon a path hidden among the trees, he turned sharply into the forest and disappeared.

.

Before the boat came in sight, sea gulls would begin to circle in front of the fishhouse and flutter down one by one to perch like statues on the rocks and wait. More followed when the boat appeared far up the shore, drawing slowly closer in the morning sunlight. When he came close enough, Peter Thunberg would turn off the motor once again and let the boat drift slowly toward the shore until with a hollow sound it bumped gently up onto the sloping rock. Then someone who was waiting there would pull it up and secure it with a line stretched to an iron cleat anchored in the rocks. I stood by idly. I listened to the hollow sound of the wooden boat, touched my fingers to the icy water on its wet painted hull, and looked into the wooden tubs inside filled with the silver, gasping fish.

Inside the fishhouse, Peter Thunberg cleaned them quickly, with rapid flicks of his brown and thickly calloused hands. He placed aside the clean slabs of meat, and the rest he pushed through a hole in the tabletop to a waiting tub below—the staring, lopped-off heads with their open mouths, the dark fins and tails, the smooth and veiny bladders and spleens. When Peter Thunberg began to hose off the wooden table, his nephew Dan would grip the handles of the heavy tub, carry it through the open double doors, and throw the guts and heads out onto the rocky shore for the gulls. Screaming wildly, they would clutter and thicken the air, swirling above his head, while at his feet their reeling shadows crossed and recrossed like the moving shadows of flames.

·

The silence stays in my memory. It is not the absence of sound so much as the presence of something else, the passage of time, lying quietly within the silence. Sun-laden afternoons of bright air and stillness. Dragonflies over the hot dirt road, suspending themselves motionlessly against the steady breeze coming off the placid blue expanse of the lake. Fog on a cool day moving toward the shore, then entering in among the silver trunks of silent birches. The muffled tone of the foghorn a mile and a half up the shore, melancholy and distant in the dead of night. My grandmother moving quietly with a hurricane lamp through the darkened cottage, dressed in her nightgown and long robe, checking that all the doors are safely locked. The ship's clock over the mantel chiming softly. Ashes settling on the grate. The quiet stirring of water on the shore.

·

After her funeral, the farmhouse was open to guests. I went outdoors and waited for cars to come down the road from the highway. As they did, I showed the drivers where to park. Before very long, the back yard was filled, and I directed the newcomers to pull their cars off to the side of the driveway. Then it was necessary to park on the road itself, and soon there were long lines of cars parked on the shoulder going in both directions from the opening of the driveway.

I walked along the line of cars on the road, then among

those crowded in the back yard. Several had been drawn there from a long distance. Three were from Wisconsin, one from Michigan, another from Illinois, still another from Iowa and one from Indiana. Inside some of them, road maps rested on a seat, or there would be a box of Kleenex or a pair of sunglasses or gloves, or a package of cigarettes left on the ledge above the dashboard. Most were entirely free of any personal belongings. Sometimes a blanket lay folded neatly in back.

I walked through the shoulder-high growth of weeds around the far side of the empty barn, then came back into the farmyard and stood for a time at the open doorway of the chicken house. My family had stopped keeping the last of the poultry only a year earlier, but already the inside of the chicken house was cluttered with discarded equipment, rusted tools, old feeding troughs, dented milk cans, salt blocks, a few dozen bursting sacks of unused stone grit. Across the gravel road from the front of the farmhouse, the neighbor's field had been turned under by the plow for the winter. I stood gazing across it for some time, dead cornstalks protruding from under the long furrows like a harvest of broken bones, and then, standing on the shoulder of the road, I began to pick up pebbles and throw them one at a time as far as I could out onto the open field. The November air was chill and entirely calm; the sun, half obscured behind thin horizontal pennants of gray and pale red, had touched the horizon and began now sliding down below the rim of the earth. In its light, the pebbles I threw landed in silence, raising insignificant puffs of brown dust on the immensity of the dry field.

One time at the lake, on the Fourth of July, my grandfather

had stood on the shore in the bright steady sunlight with a pistol. When he raised his arm and fired, there would be a small, concise report; then, some seconds later, a tiny and insignificant splash would appear a certain distance out on the blue surface of the water. We were excited by the small spectacle, and my grandfather, humorless and stern and un-smiling, dressed in his rolled-up shirtsleeves, shot the pistol for us a great number of times, in place of the firecrackers we did not have.

This memory comes to me now from a very great distance, from the small and ghostly reaches of time. I remember my grandmother standing on the raised porch of the pine cottage, one hand poised on the rail, silently watching us where we stood clustered down on the shore. She had five years more to live. At that time I had never seen the pistol before, nor did I know in what secret place it had been kept hidden all those years, a mute and private terror, bracketing together the decades.

NOTEBOOK

*Then it stopped again. And this time
it stopped even more completely than
before.*

TEN

(1953–1965)

Nothing must happen, yet does. In childhood, I loved the house in West Tree where my great-aunts Marie and Lutie Reiner lived. Visits there occurred twice a year, once on the twenty-third of December and again in August for a summer dinner on the wide porch. Norwegian tapestries hung on the walls of the living room. Books stood in formal rows behind glass-fronted cases. My aunts smiled, were pleased by visits from the children, bent forward in order to clasp our hands in the thin-boned warmth of theirs. The house was formal, old-fashioned, and calm. In the living room, chairs were arranged near the hearth, with small tables beside them and shaded lamps for reading. In the high-ceilinged kitchen three tall windows let in light from the north and east, and on the counter stood old-fashioned utensils with wooden handles and cranks. Rows of preserves lined deep shelves behind painted wooden doors. In late summer, herbs hung in bunches to dry, currants and berries bled through the bandage-white of hanging cheesecloth sacks, and, on the back porch, my aunts sorted vegetables and fruits in woven reed baskets as they took them from their garden.

I was twelve years old when my aunts died, in the year 1953, one following in her death within six months of the other. They were born in Iowa, on the grass prairie, the older of them in 1875. Until they died, when for the first time I learned the dates of their births, I had never thought of them as having lived through history, as having come from the past.

.

My father smoked heavily for most of his life, from the time he was fifteen years old until some few weeks before he died. No one else in his own family used tobacco—his father or mother, his three paternal uncles, his aunts Marie and Lutie, his brother Rolf or his sisters Hannah and Signe. My father, however, smoked through high school and college. In the many photographs that exist of him as a young man in the 1930s, a great number show him posed with a cigarette, or sometimes with a briar pipe. During World War II, he used a lightweight aluminum case for carrying packs of Camels or Luckies in his breast pocket, protecting the cigarettes from sweat that soaked through his shirt in the extreme humidity of the South Pacific, the Philippines and Marianas. For a decade after the war, during his years as a farmer outside West Tree, he continued to use this case, carrying it in the breast pocket of his khaki shirts, and lighting his cigarettes with the pocket-worn Zippo lighter that he had also used during the war. At home on the farm there were large ashtrays scattered plentifully around the house. When we visited my great-aunts, however, my father would light a cigarette, and, as the gray ash curled, cup his hand waiting for it to fall. Then Marie or Lutie would discreetly leave the room for a moment and quietly bring him a small cut-glass cup, or a thin china saucer from a patterned set that had been brought a hundred years before by the family in one of its early journeys to America from the Old World.

.

During the years that we lived on the farm, my father developed a cough that visited him regularly in the mornings. As he stood at the stove pouring himself coffee, his body would be wracked so that he would set down the coffee pot, brace his hands on the edge of the stove and, with his head bowed forward, grapple for breath. After long struggle, phlegm would come up and my father would move to the kitchen sink where, after more hawking, he would at last spit into the drain, turn on the faucet, and then inhale deeply with the relief of getting back his breath. This cough sometimes abandoned my father but never failed to return, and as the years went on it came to occupy an increasingly greater part of his life. By the time he had stopped farming and had become a part of the faculty at the college in West Tree, the cough was with him each morning and took up a good deal more of his time than it had before. My father would get up from bed, fix himself a coffee and a slice of buttered toast, then sit at his desk—an open book in front of him and a pen for underlining and making notes—and work for forty-five minutes or an hour with his cough, earning his lease for another day's breathing. During these times, my father was a figure of clenched fury, a distillation of rage, a hunched man caught by nets of bitterness, injustice, and scorn. He would speak to no one, have no one near him, answer no question, acknowledge the existence of no others, but sit solitary at his desk, his back to the room, willful and isolated in his rage and his need. In these later years, alcohol alone softened him reliably, and he increased his use of it as his cough became a visitor in still more hours of the day. I left West Tree for college in 1959, and, returning home to the farmhouse for holiday visits, I found my father drinking his icy glasses of gin earlier and earlier in the day—in midafternoon, at lunchtime, in midmorning—to help loosen the fingers of death's tightening grip at his angry and baffled heart.

·

In the late years of the 1940s and the early years of the 1950s, my parents were frightened of polio, the disease that crippled children, made them suffer horribly, and killed them by making them unable to breathe. During the hot months of the summers, the radio cited the numbers of new cases in the state each day and the numbers of new deaths. Swimming pools were closed, and beaches were roped off and abandoned. Even West Tree, though a small town, had cases of polio, and in fear of infection, my parents kept my sisters and me at home on the farm as much as possible. When we did go into town, my mother instructed us that we were to stay away from groups of people, not drink from the public fountain, never use the towels in public bathrooms.

I lived in terror of the disease, imagining that the virus had already infected the air I breathed or the food I ate, or that it swirled invisibly in the water I drank, and I waited daily for the first signs of sore throat or fever, inexorable symptoms that would mark me out as one of the condemned.

One day I hinted of this fear to my sister Ingie in an unguarded and perhaps peculiar way. We had been in the garden helping my mother pick green beans from the long rows of vines in the hot sun, and we had come into the house to get cold drinks and splash our faces with water. My mother was still in the garden, my father was in the fields mowing a second cutting of hay, and my sister Hannah, while bread baked in the oven, was on the front porch reading. Drying my face, I watched Ingie looking at herself in the bathroom mirror. She held her hair back from her damp temples and tilted her head first to one side and then the other, admiring herself, raising her chin, trying out different expressions.

Being her younger brother, and I suppose having a younger brother's typically critical view of that kind of behavior, something triggered me to say to her, "Do you think you're pretty?"

There may have been an edge to my voice, but Ingie answered—without hesitation, and with a certain superior and unruffled calmness, still looking in the mirror—that yes, she did think she was pretty. And it was then that my second question tumbled out of me, fell out into the open:

"Do you think you're going to get polio?"

Ingie answered me again with almost as little hesitation as before, and with almost the same calmness of tone. But her eyes caught mine for a fleeting moment in the mirror before she said, looking back again at her reflection:

"I'm not going to get it and I know I'm not."

"Know?" I said. I was intimidated by my sister's certainty and calm superiority, but at the same time, by its obvious wrong-headedness, it threw me into incredulous anger.

"You can't know," I said. "There's polio. People are going to get it. How do you know it's not you?"

"Someone else will get it," she said.

"Someone else?". But who? I was thinking, as usual, of myself. But my sister allotted me no safety, would not deign to include me within the charmed circle of her own immunity. She let down her hair, turned from the mirror, and went out of the room, leaving me behind with a towel in my hand and the fear of doom in my heart.

"Someone else," she said as she went past me. *"Other* people."

·

Death was to visit my family, but not through the paralyzing disease that I so much feared in those early summers. That moment with Ingie, when she was looking in the bathroom mirror, brings to me another memory of many years later, from 1962 or 1963, during one of my last visits home while my father was still alive: a summer night, gathered in the farmhouse kitchen, the doors and windows open to the darkness outside, bottles of gin standing on the drainboard of the sink. Ingie was newly married by this time, soon would be expecting a baby of her own, was no longer the pretty twelve-year-old girl so lightly confident of the security of life. She said to my father that summer night in the kitchen: Please stop smoking. Please drink less.

I remember the pretense of a bemused expression on my father's face, the sarcastic smile beneath it, and the drink-slowed cadences of his cool, logician's responses that, before they were finished, were to bring Ingie to tears of bitterness and frustration and send her in flight from the room.

"You're too young to understand the purpose of life," my father said. "Lives have only one—"

"I know the purpose of life," Ingie told him.

"Well, then," said my father, "why are you saying what you're saying?"

"Because I want you to think of us," Ingie pleaded. "Think of *others.*"

Again there was the subtle, sarcastic smile on my father's face, and again the benevolent but condescending tone in his voice as with slow patience he explained Ingie's error to her. My father was standing up—my family seemed always to stand up around the farmhouse kitchen when we drank together—and he leaned against the edge of the sink, his long legs crossed one in front of the other, his arms cradled, a gin glass in one hand.

"Ingie," he said slowly, doling out his words with a faint, calculated pleasure, "you have to understand that you're being a sentimentalist. You've simply got to think more clearly. Others aren't in a person's life. Only a single person exists inside a life. There isn't any such thing as a crossing over. I don't understand what you mean"—he shrugged with mock innocence, looked at her with paternal kindliness—"when you say think of *us*."

It was typical of my father in those years when he was bargaining with death to construct radical, threatening arguments like this one and then—filled with the capacious leisure and false bravado of alcohol—defend them perversely and explore them sinuously to the end. In the case of this particular summer night, however, Ingie broke with the tradition; she lost her temper, spat out angry words at my father. Fighting back tears, she called him mean, selfish, a liar. The outcome, though, was little different from usual. After some disruption, apologies were offered, vows of love and of no harm having been intended were made, and Ingie returned to the room, where my father continued the argument, raising it carefully to a level so theoretical that even Ingie granted it harmless enough and acceptable.

What I remember more vividly, though, is Ingie's outburst

of anger, and the look it brought to my father's face when she called him mean, selfish, and a liar. For a moment, and only briefly, I saw alarm on his face, panic, and a particularly pathetic and defenseless kind of fear, before he was able to recompose himself, step again behind his mask of cool and archly-protected logic. I did not often see such a look on my father's face. It reminds me now of the moment years earlier when I was frightened of dying from polio and Ingie's eyes met mine for that fleeting moment in the bathroom mirror, before she was able to compose herself again and tell me calmly: *"I'm not going to get it and I know I'm not."* I think that what I saw at these times was a glimpse at death, somewhere behind the briefly unguarded face, within the momentarily alarmed eyes.

.

In 1950, my grandparents sold the movie theater in West Tree and built a three-room addition, with its own kitchen and bath, onto the side of our farmhouse. Here they lived in the winter months; in the summers, from late May through mid-September, they lived in their cottage on Lake Superior. After my grandmother died in 1956, my grandfather spent one more summer at the lake, then the next summer closed the cottage and put it up for sale. After that, he lived year-round in his rooms on the side of the old farmhouse.

My father, enclosed in a struggle with his own bitterness, chose to have less and less to do with him as the years went on and grew increasingly scornful of him as the world my grandfather lived in became smaller and smaller. After my grandmother's death, my grandfather continued to drive his car to pay visits to relatives or friends on farms some distance away or in neighboring towns. But these visits became gradually

less frequent, and after a time my grandfather drove no farther than into West Tree to buy groceries or go to the bank.
In 1961, he sold his car and, after that, gave my parents lists
of groceries to buy for him. He still made his way out of the
house each morning to bring in a pail of coal for his fireplace
and later to carry out his ashes and garbage, but in time he
stopped using the fireplace and he set his garbage in a small
bag outside the back door. Then he stopped cooking almost
entirely and came to the other side of the house to take his
meals with my parents. But during these meals, my father
chose to maintain a stony silence, or else to speak sarcasti-
cally of my grandfather in the third person, as if he were not
there, and soon my grandfather stopped coming. My mother,
remaining helplessly the conciliator between my father and
my grandfather, took his meals to him on plates. Near the
time of his death, in January of 1965, he had stopped physical
movement very nearly altogether. His kitchen was unused,
his fireplace empty. He no longer went into his bedroom at
night but slept sitting up in the same easy chair where during the day he watched television, read magazines, or simply
gazed for long periods of time into the air, waiting.

.

Once he was freed of the farm—the livestock gone, the
land rented out, the barn empty—my father began buying
two-seated sports cars in which he and my mother alone
could ride, as if he wished to declare himself, his farming
years now behind him, independent once again of yet another
element of his own past. During the decade that he taught at
the college in West Tree, he traded in for a new car of this
kind each year or two. Each time, the cars became faster,
more powerful. First there was an MGA, then an Austin-

Healey, after that a BMW, and before the end my father had driven two Porsches.

He drove these automobiles hard, with a chill, concerted, and joyless pleasure that he shared with no one. The cars were his alone; no others were to drive them, or, with few exceptions, touch them. Emblems at once of escape and of calculated risk, they served a double purpose for my father; and it was a purpose—insolent, dangerous, secret—that remained his alone, that excluded all others.

·

During those years, my parents went each summer on a three-week trip by car. For months in advance, through the cold of the winter, my father planned these trips, poring over maps, considering itineraries, writing letters to motels to make reservations for rooms. The decisions he made— whether the trip was to be to the south, west, or east—were based always on the same set of requirements: the trip must not take them anywhere they had been before; it must not require them to stay in one place for longer than a night or two, at most three; and it must require them to cover a very great deal of ground. The itineraries, when my father had finished planning them, were like long pieces of string stretching out across the continent in one direction or another, looping widely, and at last coming back to the farm, with tiny, carefully spaced knots representing the stopping points after each day's travel.

My mother was not naturally a traveler, but she submitted to my father's enthusiasm for these journeys. I believe she would more happily have stayed at home, or traveled to one place to lounge at ease for the three weeks. But in deference to my father's wishes she maintained a good humor, accompanied him in his pleasures, kept a small but detailed logbook of the journey for him to put away among his other belongings at home. For my father, though, these trips were more serious; they were carefully staged rituals of escape that he approached with reverent, priestly earnestness and that he scrutinized and deciphered over and over even after they were done. With particular concern, he made certain that the trips were kept puritanically rigorous: some hundreds of miles each day in the buffeting wind of the open car, a shower, and then icy glasses of gin on the veranda of a distant, anonymous motel, a leisurely restaurant dinner, more icy gin, then up early the next morning to continue the quest.

This rigor, this fast cross-country pace, was important to him because he wanted to achieve through it the sustained exhilaration of travel—not travel toward any destination, but the condition of travel itself. My father wanted through these trips to escape from every previous association, associations even with himself, and for a brief time each year he was able to do it in this way, through high-speed automobile travel over great distances, through sustained flight. Careful never to visit the same place twice, he could be free from memory. Careful to remain always among strangers, he could be free of the burden of a prior identity, of the necessity of acknowledging reluctantly who he was. On these grueling, ritual summer trips—carrying with him his maps, tobacco, gin— my father turned his back on his family, cut ties with his own history, raced away from the following shadow of himself.

And of course there was the thin, distant, statistical element of danger that allured him as well. Hundreds and hundreds of miles at high speeds on open roads: the blown tire, the haywagon turning slowly onto the highway below a hill, the other car swerving inexplicably into the wrong lane. Any of these might have awaited my parents on the road, snatching them quickly away somewhere on the wide arc of their distant travel, soundlessly and suddenly, leaving the rest of us behind.

Returning from these summer journeys, my mother would be exhausted and worn, and yet a certain warm cheerfulness would radiate from her, revealing her relief and contentedness at being home once again. My father, though, however exhilarated he may have been on his journey, returned home sullen, taciturn, and dour. I remember seeing him standing at the dining room table, flipping with a grim, volatile distaste through the pieces of mail piled up there, not yet even having slipped from his shoulder the leather bag in which he carried with him his cigarettes and maps.

·

For a summer or two after my sisters had moved from the farm—Ingie to her youthful marriage, Hannah to work as a journalist in St. Paul—I stayed in the house while my parents went on their automobile trip, in order that my grandfather would not be left there entirely alone. My days during those times were empty and regular. I had a job in West Tree with a landscaping contractor—laying sod on lawns, planting shrubs, putting in drainage tile. When I got home each afternoon at four o'clock I showered, made something to eat, then sat through the early evening hours reading on the kitchen porch. Sometimes near sunset I took a walk around the farm—dense now with overgrown greenery and thick foliage, the sagging outbuildings all but obscured by the limbs of overarching trees and by the tall weeds and saplings that had sprung up around their foundations.

I went around the back of the barn, past the empty silo and the old cement drinking tank for livestock, cracked now and filled with pieces of broken cinder block, one side of it leaning outward as if about to fall. These were the summers of 1960 and 1961. There had been no cattle on the farm since 1952. The barn, converted after that to hold thousands of chickens, had been left empty since 1955, inhabited now only by stale dust and a few stray feathers. In the barnyard, where the cows had once clustered on summer evenings waiting to be milked, small elm trees and volunteer box elders grew, throttling one another as they reached upward for light, and around their thin trunks grew a dense tangle of acrid vines and nettles, tall ragweed and blossoming high thistle.

Sometimes I left this shadowy, early darkness and walked into the open pasture to the north of the farm, where the sun, falling low in the west, still threw its warm light over the low hills of the prairie. From the rounded crest of the second hill to the north, the highest point on the farm, I could stand and survey for a very great distance, miles and miles, to where I imagined I could almost see the curve of the horizon.

These evenings were mild, hushed, and still, with no movement of the air as the sun touched the horizon in the west and began to slide below it. I looked down at the farmstead, a low, hunched darkness of overgrowth and foliage, the buildings hidden and enshrouded by leaves and greenery. At the center of that darkness, my grandfather sat alone in the empty farmhouse, gazing into the darkening air. And my parents, hundreds of miles beyond the horizon, somewhere on the face of the republic, sped in their open car on a highway, hair tousled by the wind, racing quickly farther and farther away.

.

Hannah called me from St. Paul, from the newspaper, and I could hear shouting voices in the room behind her, and the throbbing of presses in the background. She was happy and cheerful. She would see me late Saturday afternoon, she said, maybe by four o'clock, certainly not past six. She had Monday off and could stay two days.

"I'll help you fill up the old house," she said. But on the highway halfway home the wheels of the small sports car she had bought in imitation of my father went off the edge of the pavement. Something happened when she tried to turn back on. The car fishtailed, spun around, then brushed the side of an oncoming car. From the impact, Hannah was thrown out of the open sports car and some distance through the air, down an incline and into roadside grass near a culvert.

I didn't hear about it until almost seven-thirty, when she had already been dead two hours. When I hung up the telephone, something happened to my hearing, and I thought for a moment that I had gone deaf. The farmhouse seemed to me utterly, absolutely silent. But then something else happened and sounds slowly came back to me—my own peculiar breathing, a cricket under the screen door, a dog barking on the neighboring farm. My parents were half a continent away, in a motel room in the White Mountains in New Hampshire. When I dialed them I heard the slow clicking of the trunk lines as they connected, a long moment of empty silence, then the ringing and at last the distant voice of the motel clerk answering his telephone. He asked me to repeat the names. Then there was a click and a soft hum as he rang the room my parents were in.

They came back by car, taking the most direct route possible, traveling twelve and fourteen hours a day, driven by shock and grief. I made telephone calls to Ingie, close friends, other relatives. During those warm August nights, suddenly emptier by one person, the windows of the farmhouse blazed with quiet lights and its rooms were filled with people—just as Hannah had said they would be—as we waited for my parents to come back across the face of the continent, rushing, as if they were being pulled helplessly by a long invisible string.

.

I was no longer living at home when my grandfather died, although I know that his life had changed little from the time when I was still there. After Hannah's death, badly shaken by it, he went into the hospital for a stay of some weeks, and it seemed to me that he came home smaller and more stooped, paler, and with the dour gaze in his eyes somewhat more wary, fearful, and tentative than it had been before. In letters from my mother over the next year or so I learned some of the details of this last part of his life—that he ate increasingly little, spent the days and the nights sitting up in his easy chair, chose to see no one except my mother, of whom he asked frequently and with grim humorlessness about lost names, faces, small events that came randomly to his mind from half a century before, as if he could no longer be certain they had ever been real.

My mother fed him, shaved him, did what she could to keep him clean, urged him to move more frequently from his chair, but there was little she could do to bring joy to the close of my grandfather's life. After his death finally came, my mother found a gun hidden under the worn cushion of the chair he died in. It was the same old, heavy pistol that, claiming it was for the protection of his household, he had bought in the years before the beginning of the 1920s; the same that I knew he had once wielded in jealous anger at his young wife; and the same that I myself had once seen him fire repeatedly in a humorless Fourth of July celebration on the shore of the lake. Here it was once again, nested egglike under the sitting body of the dying old man. Perhaps my grandfather had believed, simply by being still and keeping guard, that he could hold off through the presence of this old gun whatever shadowy force it was that ever so slowly, like a gradually tightening circle, was coming slowly, inevitably, and surreptitiously to seize him, just as it had come to seize the others.

NOTEBOOK

*The warm night air was fresh and sweet
with the smell of rain. Lights from the
large open doorways of the hangars
reflected on the wet apron as we walked
to where the plane stood waiting for us.
When we were inside and the door was
sealed, I listened to the rising drone of
the propellers slapping air. When we
started takeoff I watched the row of blue
lights slipping faster past the window,
then felt the sudden softness as the wheels
left the ground and the old plane began
to climb. Zoe put back her seat. She
leaned against my arm. The inside of
the cabin was lighted only by small, dim
lights over the seats. Outside the window,
lightning flickered from inside the clouds,*

illuminating the rising towers around us and the deep, ocean-floor canyons of the formations below. Under those clouds was the moistened prairie, and I thought of my parents in their farmhouse, a summer night of warm, steady rain and distant thunder, my mother grieving quietly, my father pondering at his desk, my grandfather gazing into the silent air of his room. Safely inside the old airplane high above them, feeling its soft movement underneath me as it supported us in flight, I allowed myself to imagine that we were traveling a great distance, moving away from time itself, past history, into another world.

ELEVEN

(1959–1973)

After years of staying away, I return home at last for a visit. It is early autumn of 1969. My father has been dead for two summers. I have not been a dutiful son.

·

Except for a handful of short visits, and except for a few summer vacations during college, I have been away from West Tree for a decade, since I was eighteen. Returning now, I find that my old friends, with whom I went through grade school and high school, have left as well. Stephen Bauer has moved to New York City. Peder Olvestrud has become a lawyer in Berkeley. Michael Fahey is in the army, and Ben Marlen is drifting among the cities of Europe. Joe Edwards has disappeared entirely.

My home town seems to me now like a place growing slowly desolate, a place that time is passing by. A vacant lot stands on the site where my grandfather once owned his movie theater. Grass grows in the cracks of sidewalks near downtown. An abandoned car has been left alongside the

river, tilting slowly toward the water. I imagine cornfields at
the city limits, waiting to enter.

.

I discover that Erwin Greaves is still in town and that he
has married a girl who was a seven-year-old child when I left
home for college. She is a pretty girl, although part of her
face and the side of her mouth are thickly scarred from a
childhood burn, as if a rough hand had struck her there and
left its mark. They have been married for a year.

I call on the couple in their small house near the river.
Erwin Greaves' wife is unnaturally shy when I am introduced
to her and doesn't raise her voice above a whisper. Erwin
Greaves and I stand in the small living room, facing her
where she is framed in the arched doorway to the kitchen.
Her eyes meet mine fleetingly; then she does not look at me
again. She gazes at the floor near her feet like an embarrassed child. Now and then she raises her glance briefly to
her husband's face and withdraws it quickly.

I am conscious of the sound of my own voice. I listen to
my words, and I am surprised to hear that they are pleasant,
congratulatory, and light. How pleased I am that they are
married, I say. To myself I am thinking, be kind, you are
looking at abandonment and the absence of hope. The girl is
wearing a pale blue dress with small flares of white lace at
the wrists. She wears a ribbon in her hair.

At last, as if it has followed hours of shifting, confused
sounds like wind or surf, Erwin Greaves' voice gives its signal
and releases her. "Well," he says, "Theresa is off to her
mother's." I respond to her departure with an effusion of
politeness, falling all over myself to be kind. The girl whispers
something in response, nods at me with her eyes averted,

then withdraws almost without motion through the doorway in which she has been standing. She goes through the kitchen and leaves the house by the back door.

.

I have returned to my home town looking for a mirror in which to find myself among others, to make comparisons, to see what it is I really have become. But I find that the glass has shattered, the characters in its image have fled, the place is empty.

.

A night in 1957, twelve years before my visit. Connie's Tobacco Shop is nestled in the middle of the town. In the back room, toward the river, cone-shaded lights hang from the dark tin ceiling over tables of bright green.

The night outdoors is subzero with cold. The wooden benches along the sides of the room are empty. On three of the tables the balls are racked neatly in colorful triangles under the hanging lights; at the fourth, Erwin Greaves is playing by himself. Erwin Greaves is not tall, but he is enormous. Fat swells his heavy body, and his big face leans over the table like the round face of the wind looming over the green earth. His thick fingers form an arch for the cue. When his arm moves, balls scatter and click on the table.

We stand gathered silently in the entranceway behind him. Then Peder Olvestrud tiptoes across to where Erwin is bent over the table and jabs a thumb into his rectum. Erwin Greaves jolts upright; his thick arm reaches back and beats away Peder Olvestrud's burrowing thumb. There is reckless laughter as the rest of us enter the room. Erwin Greaves is condescending and aloof and ignores us. He continues to study the table as we swirl in around him, and with a preoccupied nonchalance he raises one knee slightly and plucks the fabric of his trousers out from where it is pinched between his buttocks.

The pattern of our lives when we are in high school is to wait for others; we are always on the lookout, always waiting. One will be joined by a second, those by a third and fourth; those in turn will yearn uneasily until a fifth or sixth are added, and the group will await still others, or cruise through the town in aimless search.

One night in the summer Peder Olvestrud, Stephen Bauer and I take places on the empty wooden bench along one wall and watch Erwin Greaves play out his shots. The weather is hot and sultry, and the rotten scent of the murky river drifts in through the open back door. We light cigarettes, and the smoke from their tips curls up into the lights. Across the room from us Billy Vernon sits alone, with his skinny legs drawn up to his chest. His head rests forward on his raised knees, and he is asleep.

Billy Vernon is tall, pale, and sickly. He often misses school. He is placid, imperturbable, and mild. It is impossible to tell how intelligent he is, although he does adequately in his classes. When jokes are made at his expense, he grins amiably. He is disliked by no one. He is never discussed seriously, although he remains the subject of recurring harmless jokes. No one can imagine what he will do with his life. At high school graduation, he is the only one who has made no plans. He is often alone.

Years later, when I return for a visit to West Tree, Erwin Greaves makes up a sinister and macabre lie. He tells me that one night early in the previous spring Billy Vernon threw himself from the new concrete bridge over the river at Third Street and died from his fall.

.

My mother begins to weep. She and I are standing at the doorway to my dead father's study, looking at the large desk with its surface cleared of papers, at the chair pushed back slightly as if someone had recently risen from it.

My mother takes my arm. She links hers through mine, then presses my arm tightly against her body. The gesture and the physical closeness make me uncomfortable; I want to withdraw, but an unwilling sense of respect for the prerogative of my mother's grief prevents me from doing so. Even now I am unable to share my mother's emotion at the death of my father, and her helpless need continually to have contact with my body fills me with anger and revulsion. It seems to me that when she puts her hands on me, she is not touching me, but instead she is touching my dead father through me, as if I exist for her as a fleshly expression of him, and through me she awakens her sense of loss. I feel anger and a sense of sharp injustice in this, and my desire is to pull away from her and protect myself through physical distance. It is as though, even now that he is dead, I cannot be acknowledged for myself, but continue to live through the dictate and the defining presence of my father.

In a moment, I know that my mother will turn to embrace me, weeping more openly, believing that now at last she can share her grief. In an effort to forestall that event, I gently disengage my arm from hers, move away from her into the room, begin speaking in a subdued but unemotional tone about some of the familiar objects and possessions it contains. My mother comes up beside me, gropes awkwardly for my hand, clasps it in hers. I feel a sharp stab of pity for her, and a flood of paralyzing guilt, because I know how thoroughly I am deceiving her. She grips my hand more tightly, struggling genuinely to hold back her tears. She is being charitable toward me, and I know that the firm grip of her hand is intended to convey a motherly pride, since she believes I am overcome by grief and that I am attempting valiantly, in the stoic manner of my father, to repress and subdue it.

·

When his wife leaves the house, it seems that a burden has been lifted from Erwin Greaves. He expands, like an actor changing roles. As soon as he hears the back door slam shut, he turns and claps me on the back. "Damn it, old man," he tells me with a laugh, "it's good to see you." The stiffness and mannered formality with which he behaved in the presence of his wife disappear. He becomes fraternal and carefree, strikes up the old pose of a fat man's swaggering charm that is so familiar to me from a decade earlier when we were seniors in high school. He curses freely. With his familiar kind of caustic affection, he calls people dipshits and dumb asses. He launches into conversation about the old days with the ease of a drunken sailor carousing in a tavern.

I can see that we are going to settle in. In the kitchen Erwin Greaves mixes us two drinks, and then, back in the living room, he drops himself into one corner of the plastic sofa. There is the sound of air rushing from the cushion as his body settles down. He throws an arm over the back of the sofa, crosses one heavy leg over the other. He is ebullient. His round face glows. He is laughing. But I perceive the hint of something false in every bit of it. He is exaggerating, trying too hard. I begin to believe that he wishes I had never appeared. His enthusiasm is a mask, and he is hiding from me behind it.

•

My mother's telegram, with the news of my father's illness, reached me in Vienna the day before I planned to leave that city for the summer. Later I lied to my mother, telling her that the message had missed me, arriving in Vienna the day after my own departure.

In truth I carried the telegram with me as I drove southward to Venice, Milan, Genoa, Cannes. I had it with me in the sun on the beach in Nice. I traveled slowly, with the telegram folded carefully in my pocket like a perverse, horrible amulet, through Aix, Avignon, and Arles. I kept it on the small shelf beside my bunk as I slept on the overnight ferry from Barcelona to Ibiza. When at last I arrived at Santa Eulalia, fourteen days after having left Vienna, a second telegram waited for me in the post office in general delivery.

I found that my mother had provided me in her second telegram with the date, even with the exact hour and minute, of my father's death. In my room at the pension, I sat on the bed and read the note over half a dozen times with its cryptic, distant message, its coolly logical arrangement on yellow paper of letters and numbers. When my sister Hannah died seven years earlier, I remembered thinking to myself: *She is dead, I am alive.* The same thought came to me again now, but with an even greater kind of mute alarm; it seemed to me inconceivable that my father could have died and that I could find myself still living. I was twenty-seven years old, the year was 1968, and the telegram told me that my father had died on Tuesday, the 9th of July, somewhere during the time that I had been traveling by car from Vienna to Ibiza. At the table in my room in the pension, I counted back through the days of my journey until I came to that date. Then I counted forward through the seven time zones from Minnesota to the south of France. In this way I found that my father had died while I was in Aix-en-Provence, on the second of the two days I spent there. I carefully recalled that day. At eight-twenty in the evening, the moment of his death, I was finishing dinner at an outdoor restaurant-café on a small side street off the Cours Mirabeau. Across the street was a small tabac where before my meal I had bought a pack of Gauloises. I tried to imagine the precise moment, the very second of my father's death. Perhaps the waiter was bringing me cognac, or setting coffee down on my table. Perhaps I leaned back in my chair just at that instant, and placed my napkin on the table; or perhaps I struck a match, and, cupping my hands, lit a cigarette as my father died.

I stayed in Ibiza for five weeks, returning to Vienna near the end of August. On the island I did almost nothing. I slept late, through the cool hours of the mornings. I lay on the beaches. I read novels by Thomas Hardy, I read *Anna Karenina*, I read the memoirs of Simone de Beauvoir. What I had done was monstrous. I had lied to my mother. I had carefully pretended not to know that my own father was dying. Gradually I grew accustomed to the awesome fact of my having done these things. It seemed to me still that I felt no emotion, and very slowly, as the weeks passed, I came to believe myself able to stop fearing its absence.

·

We have a car for the night and a half-empty bottle of Four Roses. Peder Olvestrud drives because the car is his. Erwin

Greaves sits in the front seat beside him, with the bottle. In the back sit Stephen Bauer and myself.

It is a night again of subzero cold. Earlier, having no car of my own, I walk into town to meet the others. My footsteps are loud on the frozen earth along the side of the gravel road. My breath makes clouds that hang in the windless air behind me as I walk. Sounds carry great distances. I stop once to listen to the sound of a dog barking. A voice shouts somewhere in the darkness, a door slams, and after that the dog is quiet.

In Peder Olvestrud's car, we mix cola into the bottle of liquor and, passing it from hand to hand, we drive through the silent streets of the town. Sidestreets pass us like meridians. We gaze at the lights behind curtained windows of houses and imagine girls our age inside—lying in warm baths, powdering their bodies, putting on bathrobes in front of bedroom mirrors. After a time, in the empty intersections under hanging streetlights, Peder Olvestrud guns the engine so the car spins in circles on the ice. With practice, he can cause the car to spin around two or three times before it comes to a stop. We go through the town and spin in the light of one streetlight after another. For what seem like endless moments I am pressed hard into the corner of my seat. All of us know that we are doing something dangerous and criminal, and we are all very serious and say nothing. I keep my eyes on the glow of the dashlights, where the speedometer needle jumps up high on the dial each time the rear wheels break free on the ice.

·

As we drink more whiskey, Erwin Greaves grows more serious. He laughs less often, moves his body more slowly and with greater effort. He seems like a clock running down. His voice loses its hearty cheerfulness and after a few more drinks he has become earnest, almost confessional.

He tells me that he is finally getting his life squared away, getting his feet on the ground. As the afternoon goes on, he fills in the past decade of his life. Some of it I have heard already. After high school, he moved to St. Paul and went to the University of Minnesota, then dropped out after his sophomore year. For another year or so he sold children's shoes in a shopping plaza north of White Bear Lake. After that he entered a sales-trainee position with a toy company in Minneapolis. They wanted him to finish college, so he returned to the university but didn't study and was dropped at the end of the year. The toy company wouldn't take him back. By this time he wondered what to do with himself. He took a sales job with a cosmetics company and moved into an apartment with three friends from the university. One of them was a motorcycle mechanic who wanted to open a coffee house. Erwin Greaves quit his job with the cosmetics company and began taking part-time work as a waiter in the student hangouts around the university. He went into the new coffee house with his roommate and entered the business as a partner. After a couple of months the project failed. Both the roommate and Erwin Greaves went back to their home towns to look for work.

By this time Erwin Greaves was twenty-seven. Back home, he began dating Theresa. After they were married, they rented their house near the river, and Erwin got work at the condensed milk factory, pouring barrels of hot syrup into vats of popcorn to make popcorn balls for mass marketing the following winter. After a few weeks, someone returned from sick leave and Erwin Greaves lost the job. Since then he had been out of work. Theresa, he told me, found a position as checkout clerk at the local Ben Franklin store.

•

"Do you need a raincoat?" my mother asks me. Her hands linger a moment on the sleeve of my father's coat where it hangs in the closet. "A winter parka?" Untiring, she solicits me with my father's sports jackets and suits. She opens a drawer to reveal piles of folded shirts. I plead that my size is too small; I am not tall, I am smaller than my father was, and the shirts would hang on me and billow. Neckties hang by dozens inside the closet door. Unreasonably, she wishes that I would take even my father's socks and his pairs of shoes. There are leather belts, cuff links, sweaters, hats, scarves.

Patiently, I make excuse after excuse to turn down her offers of his clothing, trying to hint in as kind a way as possible at the truth of my feelings. Yet as always, she seems not to hear what I say. "You could get use out of this," she tells me, gently handling a favorite sweater of my father's. "I know you would be proud to wear it." I feel unable to tell her, without seeming an ingrate or a monster, that I do not want to be my father, that I do not want to wear his clothing, that I find myself resentful of his memory, that I believed myself abandoned by him long before his death. My mother's grief is deep, I do not want to hurt her, I have never told her these things before, and so I am tongue-tied. I make yet another excuse, and yet again my mother attributes my demurral to an excess of passion, believing that I am too deeply moved to be able yet to accept my father's clothing. She sets the sweater carefully back on the shelf, patient to wait for the time when I can wear it without grief.

After a time, paralyzed in my inability to speak openly with my mother, I begin to fear an image I see of myself leaving from my visit. I am dressed in my father's clothing, in several layers of his jackets and shirts. Ties of his are looped around my neck, his shoes are on my feet. I am ludicrous, a clown, a padded miniature of my father, dragging behind me suitcases filled with still more pieces of his clothing, legacy of my weakness and failure. My mother stands in the open door of the farmhouse, watching me move away. *How could you not love him?* she cries after me, tears streaming from her eyes, her face contorted by grief. *How could you not?*

.

I begin to perceive that something is wrong with Erwin Greaves; I discover with uneasiness that I am unable to tell when he is lying and when he is not. I find a quality faintly threatening in my old friend; it is there one moment, gone the next. His heavy face, for all its ability to change expressions, begins to seem like a padded mask. I imagine him trapped behind it, an uneasy and suspicious animal. In his conversation there is a peculiar kind of compulsion, something self-conscious and nervously cagey, not to be trusted entirely.

The sun is setting, and its faintly reddish light penetrates briefly into the small room where we sit. It touches his face. For a moment, caught in the light, his small eyes look flat, distant, and opaque; for a moment they are small pieces of black glass set deep in the backs of his sockets, surrounded by the padded bones of his face. He looks like the mask of death.

Then the light changes and once again he is jovial. We move into the kitchen, where he fixes us yet another drink.

He is expected at his mother-in-law's for dinner, he tells me, glancing at his watch, but he is not planning to go. In this remark there is a faintly calculated tone of bravado. He'll give them a call later on, he says. He goes on to explain that the best thing about Theresa is her understanding of his need for independence. It is his first direct reference to his wife since she left the house by the back door hours earlier. The reference sweeps him into a flood of platitudes and banalities. She's a great kid, he tells me. She's shy, but she's growing all the time. He is going to put her through college when he gets things squared away. The marriage is wonderful, it is the answer to everything.

On a wall of the kitchen hangs an electric clock made of molded plastic in the shape of a sitting cat. Its tail moves back and forth against the wall and its eyes open and close languorously with the passing of each few seconds. Erwin Greaves sits on one of the kitchen chairs, gives a deep sigh and raises his glass to his lips.

The job that is going to get him back on his feet is a salesman's job with a meat company. He will travel through five states, giving the district salesmen the incentive to get the company's products into the stores. Erwin Greaves will be important, the man from the regional office.

Whether Erwin Greaves is lying or not, or to whatever extent, he creates for me an image of the future that leaves me feeling hopeless and desolate. I imagine Theresa spending whole weeks at the kitchen table alone, watching the cat move its tail against the wall in electronic silence. Five states away, Erwin Greaves gives energetic lectures on the varieties of packaged meats. Theresa watches the electric cat open and close its eyes while Erwin Greaves arranges cardboard displays of sandwich meats and hangs posters of red frankfurters on plasterboard walls. He drives for long hours on empty prairie highways. His pockets are filled with pamphlets showing tinned patés and precooked sausages. His briefcase is heavy with glossy papers and the prices of ham. With others, he is hearty, robust, and overbearing. He needs to be liked, he smiles too much, he comes too close. Slowly, it becomes clear that he will not advance in his work. People find in him something overeager and excessive, faintly embarrassing, a tendency to confide too quickly, and they tend frequently to avoid him when they can. Others will find that, in his need to please them, he does not always tell the truth, and for this they will dislike, fear, and suspect him further.

•

Two days before my visit with Erwin Greaves, I meet Billy Vernon's mother on the street. Billy Vernon's mother is one of the most kindly and nervous women I have ever met. She is almost skeletal in her bony thinness, with a tall, attenuated body. Her eyes remind me of small timid animals peering out nervously from the backs of shadowy caves. As she speaks with me, her thin hands touch her face and the side of her neck, moving like tall water birds, or else they pluck nervously at the strings of the brown wrapped parcel she carries.

Standing with her in front of the Ben Franklin store, I see that grass is growing in the cracks of the sidewalk and along the edge of the storefront. The Ben Franklin store has gone out of business. The doors are locked, and boards are nailed crosswise over them. Behind the dusty display windows someone has left an open box of thumb tacks, the short stub of a yellow pencil, an empty coffee mug.

Mrs. Vernon is eager about my inquiries after Billy. He

teaches mathematics, she tells me, to eighth graders in a junior high school in Minneapolis. I explain that I may be passing through the city, that I would like to see him. I hold her brown parcel while she searches through her purse for a pencil, then writes his address and phone number on the back of an old shopping list. I look at the small piece of paper before putting it into my shirt pocket. The list reads *tuna fish, toilet paper, picture wire, lettuce, beets*. When I say goodbye, Mrs. Vernon tells me how grateful she has been to run into me. She holds my hands tightly in hers, the brown parcel tucked under her arm, and looks imploringly into my eyes.

Two days later, when Erwin Greaves claims that Billy Vernon killed himself half a year before, I find myself frightened for a moment and badly disoriented. One of the two of them, Erwin Greaves or Mrs. Vernon, is either mad or a liar. I glance over at Erwin Greaves on the car seat beside me, behind the steering wheel, and the hair at the back of my neck prickles and stirs as if it were alive.

.

When my father was alive, I seldom entered his study. I go into it now, in the odd museum silence of a dead man's room, and look around it at my leisure, free to touch its contents if I wish. In spite of this unfamiliar privilege, I touch very few of the things it contains. On his wall hang framed Navy Department photographs of a destroyer escort and a medium cruiser at sea. There is a reproduction of the signing of the Sioux Treaty at Traverse des Sioux in 1881 on the banks of the Minnesota River: in the background, Indians feast and drink whiskey. Over my father's desk is a Picasso line drawing of a young girl, small-breasted, sensuous and vulnerable with innocence, and near it is a small painting showing the ruins of a Roman temple against the light of a purple sunset. In the closet off the side of the room hang my father's overcoats, his academic robes, and, at the back, inside a plastic bag, the blue uniform of a naval officer. In the center desk drawer, which I idly open, I find an owner's manual for a Porsche 911.

As a young boy of nine or ten, I went secretly one afternoon through my father's desk, frightened desperately of his silent wrath if I should be discovered. It seems to me now a foolish and pathetic memory, and I can scarcely believe that it could have occurred so long ago in my childhood—searching through my father's forbidden belongings, at risk of punishment, for a personal bit of him that I could hold on to. In the desk that afternoon I found paper and manila folders, worn erasers, thick fountain pens of mottled horn. I found a silver letter opener in the shape of a slender dagger, and I found a small knife with a carved ivory handle. In a front corner of the center drawer, I found a small well filled with a rounded pile of old European coins. If I were to have kept anything, I imagine it would have been one of the coins from this treasure, but, an obedient child, I put everything back and kept nothing.

·

Erwin Greaves doesn't call his wife to tell her that he won't be coming to dinner. "I'll leave a note," he says, but he doesn't write one. On the kitchen table we leave the empty bottle, our glasses, a full ashtray, two crumpled cigarette packs. Our chairs are pushed back at angles from the table. We go out the back door of the house, and Erwin Greaves lets the screen door slam shut behind him. He stumbles briefly at the top of the steps, then puts a hand on the rail and regains himself. In spite of the gathering dusk, he puts on a pair of dark aviator glasses. He wears the cuffs of his white shirt turned up onto his forearms, and he walks with an exaggerated and slightly comical swagger. In his breast pocket, strained against the thin cloth of his shirt, is a pack of Lucky Strikes.

Outdoors, the air is warm and still. As he might have done when we were still students in high school, Erwin Greaves stops to urinate behind the cover of two large bushes at the corner of the house. He is talkative, digressive and rambling. He goes in and out of the past, speaking with a kind of overexcited volubility, as if he is talking against a limit of time, trying to get everything in. In the car, with a gesture familiar to me from when I knew him a decade before, he arches his back, tugs his trousers out from between his thick legs, then leans forward against the pressure of his stomach and turns on the ignition. In the west, a rising bank of clouds lies along the horizon, and the remaining dusk fades rapidly. As we cross the new Third Street bridge, Erwin Greaves asks me if I have heard about Billy Vernon. "Yes," I say casually. "Poor bastard," Erwin Greaves says by way of answer. His eyes are hidden behind the lenses of his dark glasses as he gives me the details of Billy Vernon's death. When the new bridge was under construction, Billy Vernon jumped onto the steel reinforcing rods that stood upright like a growth of spears from the new cement pilings below. One of the rods impaled him and he hung there until workmen found him in the morning.

"*God*," says Erwin Greaves, and, to my surprise and horror, he shudders visibly. But then he quickly shakes it off, his deceiving vision of madness, like a bear shaking its coat. He shakes his head, curses briefly as if to ask what hope, flicks a cigarette expertly out the car window. A week later I meet Billy Vernon for a drink in the Radisson Hotel in Minneapolis. I don't tell him the story. And now, saying nothing, I drive past the town square with Erwin Greaves and turn onto the wide empty length of the main street. Together we pull up at the curb in front of Connie's Tobacco Shop, get out of the car, go in the front door.

•

One night in the winter when we are seniors in high school, I go out the back door of Connie's Tobacco Shop, toward the river, leaving the click of the pool tables behind me. There has been a thaw. The snow is wet, and bare patches of earth show black in the moonlight. The flotsam and waste of the town are here behind the rows of stores that line the main street. There are old metal shop signs, broken display cases, the wooden bed from an old pickup truck. There are pieces of metal, coil springs, egg crates, exhaust pipes, piles of cardboard boxes collapsing under the weight of melting snow, rusted oil drums filled with ashes. I am drunk. I go to the stone retaining wall and look down at the river below me. The water is black. Pale cakes of ice drift past slowly on its surface. Erwin Greaves comes out of the door of the pool hall. A shaft of light falls, narrows, disappears as he closes the door behind him. Heavy and bearlike, he crosses the mud and snow and joins me on the wall, where he unzips his pants and without ceremony urinates into the river. As an arc of urine connects him with the waterways of North America, he asks me, for that one drunken moment transparent and intense in his seriousness: "Reiner, what's there to look forward to?" We have been drinking whiskey and beer, and I laugh, amused by Erwin Greaves' melodrama, his drinker's oratorical air. "I suppose there's just about everything," I tell him. "Yeah, sure," he says grimly. Then he says nothing, but just stands there, ludicrously holding his penis, fallen into thought somewhere inside his big body.

·

I am married a year and a half after my visit to West Tree, after I have returned again from Europe. My wife has given up her apartment on North Henry Street in Madison, and we spend the night of our wedding in a hotel on the edge of the lake. I do not know what we are going to do after we leave Madison. We have agreed to marry and leave the Midwest.

I wake from a restless sleep to discover that the air conditioner above the door is pouring cold air over us. I get out of bed and try to find a thermostat to turn it off. I search behind curtains, near doors, along baseboards. I call the desk but there is no answer. I put on pants and a shirt, go downstairs. No one is at the desk. I ring the bell, but no one comes. I go back to the room. The windows are designed not to be opened because of the air conditioning. We are slowly freezing, trapped inside the room. There are not enough blankets and we have only light clothing with us. We get dressed and get back into bed. We sleep lightly, the sterilized, scentless air chilling us slowly to the marrow. The white blankets drawn over us look like a moonscape; we are like bodies in a morgue. We get up early, well before dawn. Outdoors, the air is rich and warm and fragrant and soft. The grass is heavy with dew. The gravel of the parking lot is damp under our step. Slowly we grow warm. As we drive, my wife sleeps on the front seat with her head on my lap. We are miles away, starting around Chicago, before automobiles appear on the road in great numbers, carrying people to work. My wife wakes up. "Zoe," I say foolishly, "are you awake?" We laugh together at my foolishness. We drive around the great flat city and head eastward, aiming for the edge of the continent. We are going to New York. From there we can go anywhere.

.

My mother embraces me, weeping pitiably. Gradually, I disengage myself from her arms, and then, my hands on her shoulders, I guide her from my father's study into the next room. I sit her down at the dining room table, and I sit down on the other side myself. The table is not large; I hold my mother's hands across its surface, at least until the weeping lessens. Her hands are warm and dry, and she clutches mine in both of hers. After a time I get up from my chair and pour us each a glass of scotch over ice; I bring the drinks back to the table, then I go for a box of Kleenex, and slowly the grip of emotion breaks away. My mother dries her eyes with one of the tissues, tries to smile her thanks to me across the table. She has been telling me about my father's death. He couldn't breathe any longer, she tells me, he weakened, lost weight, had no resistance to infection, became ill. Throughout everything, he struggled for air; in the end, in spite of his other illnesses, it was as though his death was death by suffocation.

I have told my mother that I am returning to Europe, perhaps not for long. She wishes that I would stay at the farmhouse and arrange my father's papers. She wishes I would go through his desk and filing cabinets and put his manuscripts in order. There are so many, she tells me, it would mean months of work. She believes that they should be gathered in a volume and published. She tried to begin the job herself, but she was unable to recognize all of the pieces or date them properly, and she had had no idea there were so many, dating from so far back in my father's life, very nearly from the time when she first met him. Describing the effort reawakens a sting of memory, and she begins to weep again in sorrow and abandonment. I have determined by this time that I will leave my mother within days, and that I will write her faithfully.

·

In my room at the Pension Mediterranéo in Santa Eulalia, I have pinned my folding map of Europe to the whitewashed wall. A meandering line in dark pencil marks the journey that I made from Vienna to the island. I must decide within a few days by what route I will return to Austria; I give thought to erasing the pencil line that marks my previous trip, but then I decide for now to leave it there, to make no decision.

My room opens onto a small balcony looking over the sea. In the mornings I sit there in a canvas chair and read. For a month I have spoken to no one except shopkeepers and waiters, the maid who cleans my room, the owner of the pension and his wife, occasionally other tourists on the street or in bars.

The tourists are mainly British and French. One afternoon on the beach a small French family situate themselves near my blanket, a couple with two children. I find myself fascinated by this family, the father and mother reading in the shade of their umbrella, the young son playing on the sand, but especially the daughter, whom I imagine to be seventeen or eighteen years old. I find myself becoming obsessed by her. I watch her as discreetly as possible, and on subsequent afternoons I seek her out and place my blanket near where she and her family have settled down. I cannot see enough of her long, slender legs, browned by the sun, the short dark hair that curls tightly around her face, her dark eyes, the strong line of her cheek and jaw, the perfect shape of her mouth. She moves gracefully, speaks little, seems to laugh only when she plays with her young brother on the beach, kicking a colored ball back and forth at the edge of the water. One afternoon she swims in the bay for almost an hour, floating on her back, disappearing under the blue water only to surface after endless moments a great distance away in the brilliant sun. At last she comes back to shore. She passes close by me and sits down with her parents under their umbrella. Her back is straight, her knees raised from the blanket as she rubs water from her short hair with a towel. She speaks quietly with her parents, and I can hear only a few words, *"belle"* and *"pas fatigué."* Then her little brother sees that she has returned and runs up from where he has been playing in the water's edge, calling her name. She brightens when she sees him and calls back to him with grave excitement, as if with a gift that she has saved only for him: *"Philippe! Philippe! Dans la mer, j'ai vu un grand poisson!"*

I don't see her again, but for weeks after I have returned to Austria she remains in my memory. I am unable to forget her mouth, the lines of her face, the musical sound of her voice when she called out to her little brother. I begin to understand that what I have felt toward her is envy, envy so strong that it burst into love. I envy her family, I envy her brother being called out to by her voice, I envy their fortune, their contentedness with being alive. Again and again I imagine myself swimming with her in the blue bay, imagine the feel of her body in the water near mine. I watch myself diving with her beneath the sunlit surface of the water, and

I imagine seeing together with her the great fish she saw. It is there in the shifting green light, a great and ponderous presence. It gazes at us for a moment in scorn with the coldness of its steady eye, then turns away in retreat toward the unreachable darkness of the sea.

·

A dream. The main street of the town is overgrown with tall grass. The windows of the empty stores are broken, the remaining glass hanging in shards from the frames. Erwin Greaves and Billy Vernon's mother pace in a circle through the waist-high grass in the sunlight. Erwin Greaves looks down with knitted brows and a deeply puzzled expression, as though he is searching for something lost on the ground. Mrs. Vernon's face is raised as if she is giving grateful thanks to the heavens, her thin hands clasped in front of her breast. In the background Erwin Greaves' child bride stands in a blue party dress on the Third Street bridge, calling her husband's name and stamping her foot as tears of frustration fall from her eyes. Her small mouth is a gash of red. From somewhere behind me in my sleep I hear my mother weeping lamentably, torn by grief, but I cannot see her anywhere. I conclude with secret relief that she is not in the dream. But then her weeping stops suddenly. The dream continues in perfect silence, like a silent movie, and I am stricken with the new terror that I have caused my mother's death.

·

The years pass, and I become less free rather than more. I perceive that the past has not been left behind; the decisions I made during those years follow me in ways I could not have expected and against which I feel that I am defenseless.

In small ways at first, I become eccentric, abstracted, then unreliable. I lose friends, I am inward. For a time my wife leaves me, promising to return; it seems that I seek out my own harm when in reality I am seeking out the solution to my own guilt. I am visited; the dead are dead, but they are not dead.

In my need, I visit the past excessively, seeking the thin marrow in its drying bones. I think of my balcony overlooking the sea in Santa Eulalia, of my old rooms in Vienna; of the dark-haired girl on the beach in Ibiza, her arms golden in the blue bay. Other memories come and go, like sounds brought back in the echo of a seashell. I remember the scent of a dry autumn day in Minnesota when the sun-filled air is utterly still; I remember the firm touch of my father's hand, on a rare occasion touching mine; dust curled in the back of a dark closet, a hiding place in distant childhood; a small well of old European coins in the drawer of a desk.

·

August. Outside my window the city is brought to the edge of unreason by the heat. Smells of rotting garbage rise from sidewalks and gutters. Traffic passing nearby on Broadway forms an endless distant sound, like surf, or wind. On the sidewalk in front of my building, people pass by with radios playing loudly under their arms, carrying along with them slowly expanding caverns of pulsing sound. I am living alone; I admit that my apartment is not well cleaned or entirely free of smells. I have broken the mirror over my sink; pieces of the sharp glass lie beneath the gray filmy water in the basin, one or two edges protruding. In the evening I stand at a window. Darkness gathers slowly. On the tarpaper roof of the next building, across the air shaft, I see a moving figure, someone who seems to appear and disappear. I am certain that it moves, that it really is there, that it is a figure, but when I lean closer, shout something aloud, it is suddenly gone. For some time I stand at the window and stare at the place where I believe it was.

TWELVE

(1971–1975)

I

A woman goes mad early one morning. She screams in rage, shouts with a coarse abusiveness, begins throwing her possessions from a window of the building that neighbors ours. The window is on the tenth floor; perhaps it is her dining room, or kitchen. The woman's words are not always distinct, her shouts distorted by the deceiving acoustics of the high surrounding walls of other buildings.

From the window of our own kitchen I can see the things as she throws them out. A broom appears, sailing in a graceful arc like a spear, and falls ten flights to the courtyard between wings of the building. It bounces once, then lies still as death on the courtyard cement. It is followed by a dust mop, a three-legged stool, and then a box of soap flakes that, twirling, leaves a corkscrew trail in the air as it falls.

My wife comes up behind me, having been awakened also by the echoing rises and falls of the screaming voice. It is autumn. The sky is blue, and steady morning sunlight floods the side of the building from which the objects are coming. A piece of bright red clothing flutters down with a forlorn, exhausted gaiety. It is followed by coffee cups, one after

another, then dinner plates. A tray of silverware appears in
the air, turns lazily, empties out bright knives and forks that
seem to hang weightlessly for a moment, then glint briefly
in the sunlight as they fall. These objects land loudly on the
cement below. As they do so, windows begin to open. Heads
stick out.

Standing behind me, my wife grips my arm tightly. Then
she turns away, goes directly to the telephone, dials the
police. There is a pause. Then my wife says into the receiver,
"A woman has gone mad. Someone has to help her."

I don't know what happens. My wife is frightened that the
woman might harm herself, but so far as I know, this does not
happen. Perhaps a neighbor entered her apartment, came
inside to calm her. The objects stop coming from the window. The woman's screaming falls quiet. Heads withdraw,
windows close. Again there is the hum of the city, the distant
sound of morning traffic from the nearby avenue.

Down the hall, our nine-month-old baby is awake and
standing up in a corner of her crib. She is trying to talk,
concerning herself industriously with a cooing melody of syl-
lables and sounds. She laughs suddenly with a small, jumping
dance of joy and opens her arms wide when my wife walks
into the room.

.

When the baby was new, my wife would bring her into
our bed at night to nurse her, then lay her down, sleeping, between us. Unaccustomed to fatherhood, I awoke frequently from the grip of nightmares that I had rolled over
and crushed the baby. In these dreams there was a greatly
exaggerated element of fear. Sometimes there was a high
ocean wave with smooth, foamless sides. I would hear myself

screaming as I was swept upward toward the towering crest, while below me opened a vast cavern where the sea floor was sucked dry, and on the rippled sand, far below, lay the tiny curled form of our baby.

Later on came other kinds of dreams. In these, I sometimes found myself with my wife in a distant part of the world, walking on a dusty street in a Turkish town or sitting at an outdoor cafe in a sunlit Greek village. Then suddenly would come my heart-seizing realization that we had left the baby behind, sleeping, locked in our empty apartment five thousand miles away. Often in these dreams I would find myself standing at the side of her crib searching with my hands among the tangled blankets, finding nothing within their folds. In these cases I would struggle upward from sleep, working with numb throat and lifeless tongue to form a scream of terror and grief.

It would irritate my wife, the tongueless, gagging noises I made in attempting to come out of these dreams.

"What is it?" she would say in alarm, with a trace of anger, shaking my shoulder.

Then she would go into the next room and gather up the baby, talking to her gently, and bring her into bed and let her suckle. The baby's toes would curl and uncurl with the pleasure of it. I lay there in the quietness, filled with fear and guilt and relief, trying to calm the dying-bird flutter of my heart.

These dreams and others like them failed to disappear entirely. They would withdraw, stay away for a time, then return. They changed, altered themselves, continued to grow like invisible vines around my heart.

·

For a certain time, the fears come into a focus and arrange themselves around a common theme. I find that I am afraid of things that fall. I discover a fear of windows, ledges, parapets, terraces, high buildings. At night I lie in bed beside my wife and think, with the wakeful terror of the hysteric and faithless, of the floors and walls that support us unimaginably eight floors above the earth.

The elevator in our building is antiquated and unreliable. Its dark wooden carriage sways back and forth loosely between its greased tracks. Sometimes the car stops abruptly and the door rumbles open onto a rough concrete wall. I am less afraid of this unexpectedness, however, than I am of the imagined rusty cable, the sheared pulley axle, the torn anchorage. When the three of us get to the ground floor, the baby sitting in the crook of my arm, my heart is fisted, my breathing shallow and quickened, and drops of sweat have found their way down the sides of my ribs. On the street I am secretly obsessed by fears of flower pots tipping from sills, or by thoughts of granite slabs dropping from cornices, and I become lost in the strategy of huddling near the protecting flanks of the buildings. I curve my chest over the baby's head. I nudge my wife bit by bit toward the plate glass of the shop windows. Sometimes I am startled when I find that she has spoken to me, and it is necessary for me to ask her again what it is she has said.

·

We are determined to get out of debt, somehow to set aside money. My wife takes a job, and during the daytime we leave the baby with Mrs. Quinones on 97th Street, where we pay very little for her love. The baby now walks, and each morning she takes five steps across flowered linoleum to waiting arms and Spanish warblings. Mrs. Quinones' house smells of virtue and goodness, of boiling beans and cooked ham, of waxed floors, of baking cookies. But her house is kept sunless and dark. In the front room the window shades are drawn against the daylight, and the furniture stands dustless under covers of transparent plastic. A high wooden sideboard has been draped with white cloth and converted into an altar where tiers of holy candles flicker in the gloom. All day when I am at work I see my daughter's small hand reaching up for the fringe of the cloth, and I see candles fluttering toward her from the sky.

.

A building collapses downtown; without warning, its facade cracks away and slides into the street, bringing beds and dressers with it. In Central Park, lightning drops from the sky during a rainshower and strikes a tree, leaving half a dozen young children lying crippled or dead on the soft green grass at its base. In the sky over Paris, the door of an airliner inexplicably bursts open. People are sucked from the cabin and flung like scattered seeds into the air, children and small babies among them. Two giant waves strike the coast of the French Riviera. The sea draws back suddenly a great distance from the coast, then returns in two immense, high waves that sweep away people and boats and the houses of villages. I read about these things, and then, with faintly trembling fingers under the lamp on my desk, late at night, when no one will see me, I clip out the articles describing them. I collect these pieces of paper and put them in a hidden place, as further evidence that I must keep my family away from buildings, trees, airplanes, the sea.

.

(Once on the farm in West Tree, the hitch pin bounced out of the tongue of a wagon, allowing it to separate from the tractor that pulled it. The tractor, my father driving it, continued slowly up the hill on the road alongside our fenced pasture. The wagon was loaded with hay bales, and I sat perched on top of the load. It came to a stop, then began to roll backward, gaining speed.

This was in 1948, when I was seven years old. My father, lost in some reverie of his own, was unaware at first of what had happened. Moving down the hill, the space between us widening, I screamed out to him. He turned to look, stopped the tractor, and stood up, his eyes fixed on me in alarm as I moved steadily away from him. Then he called out:

Jump!

I did. I landed on grass, rolled as I hit, and came up unhurt. The wagon, nearing the valley bottom, jackknifed, tipped, and rolled over heavily, scattering bales of hay, and then came to a stop with its four tires in the air, one of them spinning lazily. This happened in the calm of a summer evening, near sundown. My father left the tractor above and came down the hill toward me. Our shadows, as we stood there together, fell away from us, thrown a great distance across the fence and over the low flank of the pasture by the red sun that was just then touching the horizon in the west.

•

It seems to me sometimes that I do not understand time. It seems to me quite clear, for example, that I do not understand where things go, once they have happened. They exist, yet they do not exist. I do not understand this. That must mean that I do not understand the passage of time. Yet I know that the wheel spun lazily, that my father came toward

me, that our shadows were flung far eastward over the low
hill.

·

On afternoons in high school when I stayed after classes—
for orchestra rehearsals, or, in springtime, for workouts on
the cinder track in front of the empty football bleachers—I
would walk to my father's office at the college to get a ride
with him out to the farmhouse. Often on these rides my father
would not speak, but remain silent, saying nothing.

His office was on the second floor of an ivied brick building
constructed near the end of the nineteenth century. Having
crossed the campus, I would walk up its front steps, their
stone worn into concavities that held lingering pools of spring
rain, and enter through the heavy wooden door with its brass
thumblatch and handle. Inside, as the door closed behind
me, the muted hush of the past settled around me, creating in
me an uneasy reverence and awe. It seemed to me that in the
surrounding silence of the empty building the sound of my
own breathing was unnaturally loud, and the dark wooden
floors betrayed me with creaks and groans under the weight
of my steps. Through open doorways I looked into empty
classrooms where gray daylight fell from high windows across
rows of wooden chairs.

Upstairs, in the back of the building, I would find my
father in his office. Having heard me coming—from the first
muffled closing of the outside door to the fall of my steps
as I climbed the groaning staircase—he found no reason to
look up when I appeared in his doorway. Accustomed, or
so I made myself believe, to my father's unresponsiveness, I
would stand there and watch him work. Most often he would
be writing, filling a sheet with lines of assiduously fine script,

or placing notes with careful precision in the margins of a printed book that lay open before him.

From the single window beside him, gray light fell into the room, leaving his face half in shadow, and falling on his hands on the desk in front of him. Long and thinly muscled, his hands moved with an unhurried deliberation over the books and papers beneath them, resting first on one, then carefully moving another. It seemed to me at these times that I saw in my father's hands the hands of my ancestors. In that silent afternoon room of the quiet college, his hands seemed to me to be in a lineage from far in the past, to be linked in a visible heritage to the sternly ministering hands of his dead father, and to those of his father's father before him, and even to his before that, extending back, as if touched by a chain of blood, to the earliest of the devout, tall, taciturn patriarchs to emerge from the ancient and misted gateways of my family. Often, standing unacknowledged in the doorway of my father's office, as if by his fierce will I did not exist, I would watch his long fingers tremble faintly, almost imperceptibly, before touching the face of a book, or—during that long, solitary, and unbroken silence—before at last lifting the corner of a page to reveal the next.

·

I should have spoken, of course—then, and a hundred thousand other times. If I had spoken, perhaps I could more easily have escaped, could have found a way more quickly out of those silent, overpowering chambers of the dead. As it was, years later, the thing that I had allowed to be created within me by my own preternatural silence rose up suddenly and seized me as if by the throat, so that my mouth gasped for air, and my eyes, filling me with terror at what I understood them at last to have seen in looking at my father's hands, swelled to bursting with tears of blood.)

•

I became afraid of knives. This fear grew. I became frightened, in coolly logical extension, of all sharp, pointed, or deadly things. Some of these were humble, some grotesque. I feared pencils, letter openers, ice picks and screwdrivers, hammers, chisels, razor blades, tire irons, heavy wrenches, baseball bats. I feared lengths of pipe, pieces of rope, sticks of heavy wood. These fears gathered suddenly, grew quickly, took me by surprise, paralyzed me in abject terror.

•

"I don't dare move," I told my wife.

"That's absurd," she said, laughing lightly. "What do you mean, you don't dare move?"

"I have to stay here, in this chair, in this room."

My wife leaned toward me. It was night; outside the windows of our apartment there was darkness. Her face was puzzled, inquiring.

"I haven't told you this before," I said. As I spoke, I began weeping, then came sobs. Something convulsed inside me, broke into pieces. "Help me," I said. "Please help me. There are knives in the house, sharp things, hammers."

My wife moved toward me, paused, then recoiled. On her face was horror.

"Get away from us," she said. She stepped backward from me. Then she turned. She went to the telephone.

•

It was not, finally, as bad as it might have been. There is a certain resilience, said the doctor. Many of the details can be left out, many are gone. With the drugs I was given it was often hallucinatory, a deep, shapeless terror, something of inconceivable height, something bottomless. In a dream I am crawling on my hands and knees in the basement of our building. The elevator has fallen and I am groping for my small daughter in the darkness. The cement floor is covered by heavy grease that turns to gouty sewage and then to the slippery viscosity of blood. I realize, in the dream, that I have killed my own child, and I curl up in the blood, weep uncontrollably, breathing the warmth of the blood, piteously, as if for comfort. But someone is shaking my shoulder, shouting from a great distance that I am still in the dream, it is only a dream. Below me is a great darkness and there is no purpose to anything. I try to die. With sedatives, I sleep for three days without waking. Afterwards, my wife comes to visit. At first she stays only for five minutes, then it is ten, then longer. After much time has passed, she sits on the edge of the bed for half an hour each day and we smoke cigarettes together. One day my wife touches my hand. Later we stroll together through the polished hallways, take elevators to the basement cafeteria for sandwiches and coffee. In time I am seldom any longer in bed, but instead I sit reading in a chair. One day after my wife leaves, I stand at the window of my room looking out. The window is high in one of the hospital towers. I look down at the wide river below, and at the great girdered bridge that spans it; as I watch, a barge moves slowly upstream, passing under the bridge, laboring slowly against the brown current. Below the hospital is a small park, hidden from my view by the dense foliage of green trees. Looking down from my window, I can see figures walking in and out of the entranceways to the park, and along the sidewalks lining the wide avenue. At the busy intersections, people gather in small groups, waiting for the traffic lights to change. It seems to me infinitely moving that when they cross, they hold tightly to the raised hands of their small children.

II

After this, the gentle tedium of slow repair, tentative steps, the pleasure of breathing. I move from room to room, living still among ghosts, learning gradually to overcome my fear. Or perhaps they are not ghosts. And perhaps I am not really living among them. Perhaps I can clarify at least that much. But I know that there are rooms, if empty—beneath me, behind me, extending in a long corridor backward, beyond my own birth, beyond memory, farther than I can see.

•

I am visited by new dreams, some of them complicated with detail, others bare with plainness. But the immense, glass-green side of the rising ocean wave is gone.

•

In one of the new dreams, I am reading in the living room with my wife, wearing only a bathrobe. It is night. The apartment is quiet. The telephone rings in the other room, and I rush to answer it, believing as usual that it may be an emergency. It is a call from my parents. Their voices come to me as if from a great distance away. The line is filled with the crackle of static, and with high, thin, wailing sounds that rise sinuously and fall away, then rise again. There has been a heavy snowfall. My parents are snowbound in the old farmhouse. The sounds I hear, my mother explains to me, are the sounds of the wind.

"But you must be certain you don't come and help us," she says. "After all, we're alone. After all, we're helpless."

"You say one thing and mean another," I tell my mother. "I don't know what you mean," I tell her. "Do you need help? Should I come and help?"

"Don't misunderstand," she says. Her voice is faint with weariness, like a sigh. "After all, your father has asked me to tell you the same thing."

Then my father speaks. I realize that he has been on the line all along, listening silently.

"Your mother is only telling you the truth," he says. "Of course you mustn't come to help us. You should know that by now. We're suffering. We're alone. The prairie around us is windswept and immense. You know what that is like. We have no food."

Then his voice quite suddenly changes. It rises swiftly into a kind of thin, incantatory song, and I imagine his face raised upward, his eyes squeezed tightly closed, as, in a thin tenor voice, he begins reciting Latin, a long stream of smooth, roundly articulated, flowing words.

I find, in the dream, that I am filled suddenly with great anger. I interrupt my father. I shout at him, *Speak so I can understand you! Tell me what you are saying!* I take breath to say more, but after my own words there is nothing in the telephone but the sound of the empty wind. I go back into the living room and tell my wife that I must travel to Minnesota because my parents are alone in the storm. Her voice is kind and gentle, but when she speaks she does not raise her eyes from the book she is reading. "I know you have to go," she tells me, "but you don't have any clothes." I search through

closets and dressers, but I find all of them empty. Other than
the bathrobe I am wearing, it is true, I have no clothes.

This must mean, I decide, that I have just been born.

.

With the diligence and care of a student, I move through
a museum of deaths, noting each of them carefully, one after
another. There are many of them; and although I am unable
to see the deaths themselves, since they are gone, I find symbols near them, things, in the way of museums, remaining
behind and invariably suggesting absence—a piece of colored cloth, a few bright images briefly glimpsed, a gleaming
jewel set into a piece of drying bone. There is, for example,
a lake, vast and blue on a warm summer day, the air hushed,
a sea gull flying in silence across my view. A farmhouse door
slamming. A train pulling into a station, the release of steam
from under its wheels as it comes to a stop. A girl on a swing,
dappled sunlight crossing her white dress as she moves forward and back. A bedroom window, its curtains billowing
gently outward from a soft breeze. The sound, briefly heard,
of children's voices from some distance away.

As I continue in my study of them, it seems to me that certain of these deaths have about them their own colors. The
death of my great-grandfather, who came from Europe, has
about it still the deep, white-crested green of a North Atlantic
crossing in the winter months. His numerous children, born
on the nineteenth-century prairies of Iowa, sun-roughened
and tall, carry with them to their deaths the summertime dust
and gold of ripened wheat—except for my grandfather, my
father's father, prairie-born man of God and facer of death,
whose color, from his dark clothing and darker words, was

black. And the color of my father's own death, to my surprise when I first discovered it, was white. This color may have had its origin, I came to believe, on a quiet summer afternoon in 1930 in West Tree, when my father, as a young man, stood on the wide green lawn behind the house where he lived and smiled for the camera. On what occasion, I do not know. But with his white shoes planted firmly in the grass, his hands resting in the pockets of his pleated white trousers, his white jacket loosely buttoned, his head tilted slightly, almost jauntily, to one side in the sunlight, he gave his familiar, enigmatic, faint, mysterious smile, and was captured, in that pose, forever.

.

How strange, it seems to me now, how piteous and very strange, that the color of my father's prolonged and fiercely contended death should be white. Or how strange, perhaps I ought to say, that I should be able to imagine it so; or that I should be able, at last, to understand the propriety of leaving him there now, just so, standing in that sunlight, smiling, surrounded by the warm air of that long ago afternoon, in that place, on that lawn.

And having left him, I imagine him there still, timeless, patient, unchanged, waiting. But of course that is not so, of course he is not there. I have grown to understand with certainty that the past exists. The same, I understand also, cannot be said of the things in it.

.

The season once again has come to be spring, although early, the month of March. My wife and I and our children are to go on an outing. We bundle up in sweaters and jackets and caps. Around our necks we wrap warm scarves. When we go outdoors, I walk holding my daughter's hand. My wife walks beside us, pushing the stroller in which our new baby sleeps, her hands curled on the blanket she is wrapped in.

In the park along the river, an old woman has been feeding pigeons, scattering bread crumbs on one of the walkways ahead. I see her moving away, a small bent figure in rags of drab gray and brown, trudging slowly over the crest of a low hill among the trunks of bare trees. As I watch the old woman disappear, my daughter pulls suddenly free of my hand and runs ahead of me. Leaping and dancing, waving her arms, she runs happily into the midst of the feeding pigeons.

If it were possible, I would record that image, for its carelessness and joy, the life held within it. My daughter's arms are raised above her head. Her face is thrown back in laughter. Her small legs, having pushed her upward, have not yet returned to the earth. And, in a dense flurry all around her, the startled birds rise up, striving on beating wings, and fan outward into the sky.

About the Author

Eric Larsen was born and raised in Northfield, Minnesota, and educated at Carleton College and the University of Iowa. He now lives in New York City and teaches at John Jay College of Criminal Justice. His fiction and nonfiction have been published in many magazines, including *The Nation, The New Republic*, and *Harper's*. *An American Memory* is his first novel.